# The Familiar

## A Paranormal Romantic Comedy
## Bad Tom Series: Book One

## Jill Nojack

IndieHeart Press

Kent, Ohio

The digital version of this book is published by Kindle Press as a Kindle Scout winner. The paper version of the book is published by IndieHeart Press

Cover and interior designed by IndieHeart Press.

www.jillnojack.com

Publisher's Note: This is a work of fiction. Names, characters, places, and incidents are a product of the author's imagination. Any resemblance to actual people, living or dead, or to businesses, companies, events, or institutions, is completely coincidental.

The Familiar / Jill Nojack. -- 1st ed.
    ISBN: 978-0-9911234-5-2

BACK WHEN HER SKIN was smooth and her lips were juicy as ripe berries, Eunice did the nasty with the devil. And she loved it. If she hadn't, I wouldn't be lurking in the dark, twitching the tip of my tail, trying to keep an eye on what the old witch is up to. Everyone knows spells cast during the Black Moon aren't illuminated by the Goddess's light.

The candle flames bob toward the ritual grounds. I track their yellow-orange trails through Corey Woods into the clearing where the scuffling of witches' feet has worn a ring of bare earth in the new spring grass. Tonight, the coven within a coven that is loyal to Eunice gathers. Four witches. One perversely devoted warlock. And me; a small, black, feline familiar. I know better than to get too close. I know what will happen, what always happens, the same way it's happened across all the years. Why singe my whiskers?

The witches extinguish their candles when the circle is complete. Their black-robed figures are an inkier spot in the midnight. From where Eunice stands in her position of power, an even blacker tendril snakes toward the others, making the gloom appear gray in comparison. It weaves a net around the chanting witches, bending as it goes, to trace the outline of their bodies until the threads pull tight. I hear the dull thuds as all but the warlock lose consciousness and hit the ground. Protected by her favor, he moves closer to his priestess until they are cocooned together by the magic. The ebony tornado enfolds them as it swirls into the sky. The wind howls.

And then, exactly as it always happens, it happens. A bright purple orb of light streaks from the heavens and explodes inside the funnel, dispersing the darkness and tossing Eunice and the warlock backward as easily as a twister tosses a scarecrow. For a moment, they loll like turtles on their backs, their limbs waving in the air that still sizzles with violet static as the lightning dissipates.

When they recover their wits, the man flaps his palms at spots where the arcs of power ignited his robe. Eunice sits up, raises her head, and screams her rage at the retreating brightness. The year, the chant, the participants, each of them changes, but it doesn't matter. Someone powerful doesn't want her spell to be cast.

Still, like me, my mistress can't let go of the hope

she'll wake one day and the rules of her universe will have changed.

***

When the warlock is done slapping at his robe, he pushes back his hood and reveals a pock-marked face under a disheveled comb-over: Eunice's loyal sycophant, Kevin. Eunice brought him in to her Black Moon nights twenty years ago when he was just a pimply faced high school senior.

Kevin looks down on her where she still sits near a patch of scorched grass. Through compressed lips, he says, "You promised it would be different this time!"

"Just give me a hand up." She extends an arm. He doesn't take it. "Now," she adds. He continues to glare for a moment and then bends over to grasp it, helping her struggle to her feet.

His voice is low and angry. "I'm sick of your promises. I've kept the cops and Dad away from a lot of things for you. It's time for you to give me what you owe me. I'm tired of hearing just one more thing needs to happen first."

"Shut up, Kevin!" She inclines her head toward where the movement of the other witches indicates they're waking up. "Our secrets are our secrets. We'll talk later."

"No. I want my due. I want the coven, my piece

of your imports, and I want Ca..."

Eunice flicks her pinky finger at him, and his flapping tongue swells to fill his mouth, preventing him from finishing his sentence. It looks painful and vaguely obscene.

His eyes move from anger to pleading as the back of his throat closes. I try not to remember how that feels from my own experience annoying Eunice.

"Cat, I know you're there. Come out!"

Oh, so that's it. It's me who's not allowed to hear what he has to say. She always sniffs me out. I lope forward briskly, hoping to avoid the treatment her other pet is getting.

As I rub my cheek against her leg in greeting, Kevin goes to his knees.

"Will you hold your tongue?" she asks him. Her lips twitch into a smirk at her own dark pun.

He nods frantically. She waves a hand toward him as she pivots away. When his tongue shrinks back into his mouth, it reminds me of a snail pulling into its shell.

"Good. As I said, we'll talk later." She doesn't glance back at him, just starts a slow trek along the path through the woods. The chilly night air is never a friend to her knees. I think about pouncing on the hem of her trailing robe, but then I think better of it. I turn back to watch Kevin where he kneels, leaning heavily on his hands, still trying to catch his breath. He raises his head, and I meet his gaze as he glares after us with bloodshot eyes.

That's right, buddy. Look who's the favorite now.

THE NEXT DAY, it's business as usual. I'd like to take a nap, but Cat is distracted by everything: a passing shoelace, the shop broom moving across the floor, the sound of paper bags crinkling.

*Crinkling.* First my ears and then my eyes are drawn to the source of the sound. Eunice's granddaughter, Cassie, plops a brown paper bag onto the counter, and it rustles again as she rests a dainty hand on it.

"Thanks for the pickles, Gran. You know how Dan loves them. You're sure there's nothing else before I go?"

"I'm fine. Run along."

"I'm not convinced," Cassie says, turning her head to the side, her brow pulling downward, her pale blue eyes narrowing as she scrutinizes her grandmother's face. "You don't look well to me."

"Just off my feed. Nothing to concern yourself

about. Back to Boston with you, and don't forget the pickles." Eunice pushes the paper bag toward her. It makes the scrunching noise again. I try not to let the sound excite me, but it does. My haunches tingle. I want to spring.

"Okay, but call if you need me." She leans over the counter to plant a kiss on Eunice's withered cheek with her full, candy-pink glossed lips, then turns and leaves the shop, her long brown hair swaying gently across her back as she goes. If she'd been wearing stockings on those shapely, skirt-clad legs, Cat would have been off the counter like a shot to shred them for her, taking me along for the ride.

I track her departure until I spot an iridescent, feathery pigeon strolling along the back of a bench just outside the plate-glass window where Eunice showcases her magical wares. My entire being follows its every movement, lust for the hunt rising, but I'm trapped inside and can't get to it. I can only stalk it with my eyes as it struts along beyond the display of colorful potions and powders.

Another day, I'll tear into that pigeon: I have hope. I have nothing but hope. The hope I'll someday be a man again is the only thing that keeps me from running out my nine lives one after the other after the other.

But no matter how much hope I cling to, I won't be having pigeon dinner today. The swaggering bird shifts on its perch, flicks its tail, and drops a load of splat on the bench before flying away uneaten.

That's what you get with hope.

My ex-wife Gillian interrupts my bird-watching the next time the shop bell ting-a-lings. She strolls in, disappears behind a shelf, then reappears with a jar in her hand. She heads for Eunice, who's been glaring at her since the door opened, and holds the jar outstretched for her to see. From where I lounge next to the cash register, I can't tell if it's vervain or bat wing.

Good. It's time for the weekly skirmish. Although Gillian is a powerful witch, she's never been invited to my mistress's rituals beneath the Black Moon. She and Eunice are worlds apart as witches go.

"Eunice, what are you asking for this?"

"The price is on the bottom. The same place it is every time you ask."

Gillian turns the jar over and lets out a low whistle.

Eunice responds, "Go to Salem if you have a problem with the prices. They cater to the drugstore witches over there."

"You've always been an opportunist!" Gillian replies in the remnants of her British accent. The wording never changes. My sweet Gilly has become a creature of habit.

"And you're a fat, old witch," Eunice reels off from the tape the two of them have played over and over again through the years. She's a creature of habit now, too, although her accent has become more refined over time. To hear her, you'd think she's one of Boston's Brahmins. She certainly wants the residents of our dysfunctional hamlet to think so.

I only half-listen these days, particularly when I've got a good groove going with the paw-lick / ear-swipe combo. The fight never varies much. Over the years, they've both frozen into their own idealized versions of themselves. Gillian's colorful, long skirts swish along the ground enticingly, and her flowing embroidered tops make her look approachable but sloppy. She still wears her white hair long, but most days she twists it and holds it up with a clip on top of her head instead of letting it hang loose down her back. Eunice is a sharp contrast: she's all lines and angles in tailored, beige perfection with short, carefully mussed gray hair that frames a face weighed down by frowns.

"Phhht!" Gillian sounds like a leaky basketball. "Fat old witch? As if that's an insult in a town full of aging practitioners. You've always had to have your own way. You've never once considered the feelings or needs of anybody else."

"I considered Tom's feelings, didn't I? I considered them on the sofa, on the chaise, on the floor, and, obviously, on the bed." Eunice turns away from Gillian then, enjoying her own cleverness, a sly smile stretching the skin on her lips to near-transparency as she scratches seductively behind my left ear. She continues, "Sometimes I considered Tom's feelings two or three times in the same night." I push Cat to resist her, show Gillian a little silent support, but you can't imagine how satisfying a good ear-scratching is: it's sex and rum wrapped up together with a side order of pecan pie. Cat leans our head in to her hand and rubs our cheek hard against it before she turns away to face her opponent.

It's off to the races then: in their younger days, it might have ended in hair-pulling or face-slapping, although it never turned into a legendary knock-down, drag-out, winner-take-all event. Gilly always backs off after she spits out the real reason for the argument, which has nothing to do with vervain or bat.

"You drove him away, Eunice. You drove my Tom away. I'll never forgive you for that!" Then she storms out of the shop without another word, the shop bell ringing harshly as she exits. From behind a steadily grooming paw, I can see she's slowing down. Her storm is now more of a light drizzle.

Poor Gilly. But Eunice didn't drive me away. I'm still right here, hoping you don't someday push her too far and bang! Pudgy Gilly shrinks to pudgy toady, hopping away from Eunice at the end of a broom as she shoos you into the street.

I'd always hoped Gillian would recognize me somehow, but no one has ever put together my disappearance with the arrival of Cat in Eunice's shop. Not Gillian, not even that bastard Robert, the other warlock Eunice was keeping time with back in my day. She lost interest in him quick enough once she had me to herself. But why would anyone put it together? Who could believe it was possible for Eunice to have so much power?

Eunice says they've long suspected it, even hinted at it, but Gillian and the other coven members have never been able to prove she's dipping deeply into the black arts pool. Pushing the boundaries of white magic, maybe. Stocking questionable items in the store, definitely. Nevertheless, the summer tourists passing through Giles on their way to Salem expect to see "black magic" items in Cat's Magical Shoppe. It doesn't mean they're in use. It will never prove she's lying down with demons.

*\*\*\**

"Tom, come to bed," Eunice calls from upstairs now that the shop is closed. I'm still downstairs with the shadows, pouncing away at the ones that take my fancy, but I always know what's coming after a day like today. There are few surprises between us after over forty years of our arrangement. Tonight's the night. I can feel it. A run-in with Gillian always revs her up.

"Now, Tom!"

There's nothing else I can do. I climb the stairs one slow step at a time, but I only delay the inevitable. I pad into the bedroom and jump lightly to the bed. Cat's body ignores my heavy human heart. She reaches out a hand to stroke my back, and Cat arches in response, purring softly despite my reluctance.

"Good Tom," she says. The magic words.

I'm used to the change they precipitate now—the pain, the near loss of consciousness, being suddenly disoriented in a world full of the reds a cat's eye can't see.

Here I am, Tom Sanders. Naked, chilled without my fur, and resigned to what comes next.

Understand that she never forced me. I've always yielded. And it wasn't so bad forty-five years ago. It's in both my and Cat's nature to yield to a woman without too much fuss, and Eunice was a breath-taking woman in her day. But Cat and I only age in proportion to the time we spend in our own forms, and I've been mostly Cat for years. My body is 24 or 25. My soul, if I still have one after doing Eunice's dirty work for so long, is much, much older. By the time I finally realized satisfying every woman who asks isn't what makes a man a man, I found myself no longer man enough to care.

Eunice turns where she sits on the edge of the red satin bedspread and extends a fairy-pink shot glass toward me. "Catnip, Tom." It's an order.

I could refuse her. I want to refuse her. There's nothing erotic left for me now that she's over seventy. She'd be angry and punish me in other subtle ways, but she wouldn't force me. And she doesn't approach me often now. There are times, when she's in a rare mellow mood, I even feel sorry for her. She's as lonely as I am. No one but Cassie loves Eunice.

I knock the potion back. It tastes sweet as it goes down, but the aftertaste is bitter. Things blur. Under the influence of the aphrodisiac, I move to her, seeing her as she looked forty years ago. My hands drop to her waist, and I pull her toward me. In my bewitched state, her body yields with a flexibility she lost long ago. I let my lips trail downward from her earlobe to her collarbone, and now it's Eunice who purrs.

***

As the potion wears off, it leaves my mouth dry and my left eye tingling. The sensation of Eunice's slack skin beneath the cradling arm where I'd felt the firm flesh of youth only seconds before gives me a jolt. And there's that subtle odor she's developed over the past few weeks: a whiff of bowel overlaid by a definite top note of decay. With my head unmuddled, I regret I didn't stand up to her. I can't linger tonight in some vile imitation of affection.

She turns and reaches for me. I shrug away. "I don't want to snuggle. Turn me back into Cat. I'll sleep in my basket." I roll across the bed and put my feet on the ground, preparing to walk away. It feels good to talk back to her.

"I'd think twice, Tom. You've managed to keep Cat intact in this lifetime. That doesn't mean a visit to the vet is out of the question."

Oh, there it is—the big threat—neutering. It affects Cat but not my human body: that wouldn't suit her at all. But it makes Cat docile and loving. It makes him lose interest in the hunt. It makes him rub up against her legs whenever she's near like she isn't hellspawn. And me? It makes me want to run him in front of a swiftly moving train.

I think about the snip, and I flash to the memory of her ancient body pressed to mine insistently only moments before. I can't care about the threats any more. I'm done. In this moment, I'm done hoping. I can't care about anything.

I'm up and running away toward the window when the silver sparks twine around me, entangling me in a net built with strands of her magic.

She gets out of bed. Her robe rustles as she walks toward me. She moves in front of me where I can see her and says, her voice low, "Four more lives, Tom. That's all."

When she's calm like this, it scares me more than the rages.

"Do you want to go out, Tom?"

I can't move, so I don't respond.

"I know you do. But you want to be wearing this fine, manly body of yours when you leave, don't you? You could walk over to Gillian's and tell her how sorry you are you cheated on her. Or take flowers to your mother's grave, perhaps?" She leans in to my ear, solicitous. "It was sad you missed your parent's funerals. Or no—you could escape Giles altogether and go back to your tomcatting ways in the big city. I think that's more likely, don't you?"

She turns and walks into the hall, and I'm pulled along behind by her magical, silver tractor beam. I struggle not to lose my footing on the stairs as it tugs me downward.

When we're finally standing at the shop door, looking out on the deserted nighttime street, she frees my head and neck, then places a hand on my jaw to turn my face to hers. She gives me an unpleasant smile. "Go on, Tom. I give you your freedom." Her voice drops to a whisper. "Walk out like a man."

The magical net lets loose. I face forward, close my eyes, and take a deep breath. I know I can't leave as a man. I know it's a trick. I know she's taunting me: this hope welling up inside is just another load of splat. Every door, every window, every point of exit from this house precipitates the shift.

But I can't help it. The same as my mistress, I can't bear to let go of the hope that one day I'll wake up and the rules of my universe will have changed. I'm not thinking of the transformation any more than Eunice thinks of the spell-shattering bolt of brightness under the Black Moon. I'm thinking only about how the wind would feel blowing through my hair.

I open my eyes and step through the doorway. I'm outside, and I'm Tom. And the breeze, oh the breeze…

Then the pain comes.

My body pulls in on itself, folding up like intricate origami, my smooth skin darkening and sprouting fur, until Cat stands where the man was.

I hate myself for believing, even a little.

Eunice's laughter follows me all the way down the street.

***

Cat doesn't like fog. You'd think he would with both he and the fog ghosting around on their little cat feet, but despite the potential for stealth, it hides the small movements of nearby prey. Hunting is poor. I hear the night creatures scatter as they smell me moving toward them, but I can't find them. They're lost in the mist.

I prowl the backyards of the row of well-maintained Victorian-era buildings where the shop is located, searching for a creature skittering there that I can stalk and control and kill. But there's just the rustle of small feet hurrying out of my way. It'll be off to the woods, then. I can sniff something out farther from home. Maybe a squirrel, something that isn't afraid of a fight.

I dart across the street, distracted by my urges. Tires squeal ten feet from me. I look up at the driver and see good ol' Kevie-baby's ugly mug in the windshield just before Cat is knocked over and goes down screaming to be crushed by a rear wheel and pop out behind it in a world of pain.

I'm too hurt now to even scream as the car pulls to the side of the road. I hear doors slam and raised voices.

"I don't know why you always have to make a big deal out of everything, Dad. Leave it for the road crews."

"We're not leaving some kid's dead pet on the street where he can find it. Toss me your keys. Do you still have those burlap bags in the back?"

Great. Robert's here, too. If I wasn't already dying, Eunice would kill me.

There's a jangling thud as the keys hit the road, and a little later, the sound of the trunk popping open as footsteps move toward me.

Then the pain stops, and the breath stops, and the sound stops, and the dark starts, and I'm in that nothing space where I know I'm dead. I wonder idly if it's final this time. But no, it's only Cat's sixth life done: the transformation begins.

It happens fast. Claws retract as fingers grow, fur becomes hair, the bones in my legs crack as they stretch and straighten and push their way out.

For a brief moment, I'm a buck naked man in the middle of the street, blinking at the brightness of the streetlight after the darkness of death. Brief, yes, but it's long enough for Kevin to spot me as he walks back to what he thinks will be a cat's carcass he's supposed to bag and take to the dump. When he sees me, his eyes go round, and the curse he utters isn't a magical one. Then the cat comes back as my body folds into itself.

Yes, Cat's back as a sweet young kitten.

I can't resist a quick kitty-wink at Kevin before I run into the woods.

THE WOODS ARE LOVELY, dark and deep, just like that poet wrote it. But I'm no longer a bad-ass tomcat with years of muscle memory for hunting and killing. I'm a mewling kitten that could barely take down a mouse, much less a gigantic squirrel. The woods, which should beckon freedom, shout out danger now. I crawl into a hollow at the base of a rotten tree to sleep there, dozing then waking, wary of the night noises. An owl hoots in the distance. I cower in my hole.

In the morning, I run home, tripping once or twice on my tiny, newly unfamiliar feet, and glance both ways before I cross each street. I bet it looks cute as hell. I hate it when Cat loses a life.

When I arrive back at the shop, I shimmy up the tree in the back, move along a branch that leads to the open window, and launch myself at the sill. I snag it with my front paws, but as I dig in for firmer purchase, I feel like I'm posing for that poster from the seventies—the one with the cat and the branch and the "Hang In There, Baby." I slide down the sill fast, losing my grip and hoping my young bones bend instead of break when I hit the ground two stories below.

Then, I'm traveling up and in by the scruff of the neck. As Eunice saves me, she starts in. "Stupid, stupid Tom. Another life gone? That only leaves seven, eight and nine, and you could have just lost number seven." She drops me on the floor, not gently, and I skulk away under the bed to spend the morning in hiding.

I wish I didn't have to return, but where else would I go? I don't want to live the rest of my lives trying to make my way as a mangy alley cat. Maybe it's time to accept I'll never be a man again. In fact, with this latest setback, I'm not even a decent cat.

\*\*\*

I wake to the sound of a ringing phone, which Eunice answers promptly.

"Cassie, stop crying. You're worth ten of him, sweetheart," Eunice murmurs into the phone in the deceptively kind tone she saves for her granddaughter. I hear the girl's sobs from where I'm still hiding under the bed.

When she talks this way, a listener might think Eunice truly cares, but her interest in Cassie, like her interest in anyone, isn't genuine. She wants something from the girl. I know it, and I want to protect her from it, but I've never been able to figure out what it is. Still, she's been over-solicitous of her granddaughter's well-being since she was eight or nine. Cassie had been hit by a car, and Eunice not only donated blood, she stayed by her bedside for days. From then on, Cassie stayed with us on her summer vacations. She was someone nice for Cat to cuddle with. She never demanded more than I wanted to give.

"No, dear, no, you don't pack his things up for him nice and tidy. You found him in bed with your best friend! No, his things go on the lawn. Preferably in the rain, with the crotch cut out of all his pants...that's the only thing for it, dear. Are you listening? Go find the scissors now before you forget. I'll wait..."

Ten minutes pass while Eunice waits. "Lovely, dear. How did it feel? Yes, I said so, didn't I? Granny Eunice always knows what to do...and remember, on the lawn once you're finished. He needs to know that final is final. He'll not be forgiven, not by you. Not ever."

Eunice makes her goodbyes and places the phone back in the cradle as a smug expression plays across her face. She airs her thoughts out loud, perhaps to herself, perhaps because she knows I'm still lurking under the bed.

"I cannot believe that disaster zone of a girl

found someone to get engaged to and nearly ruined everything! In any case, that's sorted things nicely, if I do say so myself."

She walks through the hall to the small kitchen/breakfast room combo at the end. She calls out, "Cat!"

I don't have a choice. My cat self has a painfully empty stomach due to being freshly reanimated and cowering in the woods all night, and while I might regret it, I sweep out from under the overhang of the bedspread, stopping only briefly to bat at the fringe, and then rush along the hall toward the sound of the can opener and the smell of something savory. I leap from the floor to the chair to the tabletop, where my blue ceramic dish contains a pile of fishy-smelling slop. I eagerly shove my little pink nose into it and chew away daintily as Eunice rubs me behind my tiny black ears and waits for the kettle to boil.

I hate myself for purring. Cat forgives everything so easily when food is involved.

"Well, Tom, I'm sorry that you can't join me for tea. I prefer the company of Cat right now, given your behavior last night. Such a shame you're not always as sweet-tempered as a kitten."

I glance up from my meal, and she gives me a quick scratch under the chin. "You do look charming. Perhaps I'll leave you that way, and you can go fully cat from now on." She's a shark when she smiles. "How would you like that, Tom?"

I try to arrange my face into an expression of horror, but I'm sure my wide-open eyes and plastered-back ears just make me adorable. No, I wouldn't like being fully cat from now on. Every time I'm Cat too long, I start to lose my human self.

The last time Eunice forgot to let me spend time in human form, I almost didn't come back from it. She was having her brief but unsavory affair with Kevin after school in one of the cabins she owns in Corey Woods. She was in her late fifties at the time. Despite Eunice's trim figure and piercing blue eyes, young Kev must have been one hard-up teen to do it with a woman old enough to be his granny. And Eunice? I've never been able to figure out what she'd want from such a soft, greasy chunk of high school wedgie bait.

It was a week, at least, before she got the itch for me again and sprang me from Cat's body. I held her immobile with my teeth gripping the back of her neck, and she arched, scratched, and growled when I treated her to a little lovin' the tomcat way. Later, as we lay together, perspiration shining on our exhausted bodies, she rubbed up behind my ear with one hand as if I were still Cat, and said, "The teeth were a nice touch."

Despite her approval, there's no way she'd want me asserting myself *outside* of the bedroom. She never left me as Cat that long again.

"Something special today, or just the usual, Robert?"

Although he keeps his eyes on Eunice, I can tell he's aware of me playing possum on the top of a shelf with one eye cracked open.

It was a long time ago, well before he fathered that mess of a boy who turned out to be Kevin, but Robert was my rival for Eunice's romantic attention. The two Andrews men couldn't be much different. Robert is dapper and well put together. He's never gone in for the casual style that's so popular these days. Even now, when he's just out shopping for herbs, his crisp cotton suit is perfectly tailored to fit his tall, thin frame. If I'm any judge, he's still handsome for an old man.

Although he never progressed in magical power to a point that allows him to challenge Eunice in spell-making, he's been the high priest of the coven for twenty years and the mayor for longer than that. Between the two of them, they own most of Giles. I'm convinced he hopes to increase his share when she's gone—if not for himself, then for his psycho son. Giles is an insulated place. Exactly the kind of town where bad magic can really get a claw in.

"I'm thinking about trying something new for pain. The arthritis has been at me. New kitten?"

"Indeed. Out with the old Cat and in with the new. The last one met up with an accident, but there's never any shortage of black kittens available."

"When did you get the first Cat, Eunice? Maybe Kevin could work up a piece on your shop for the Free Times. Might bring in a few summer tourists hoping to take a peek at the famous Cat."

"It was in sixty-seven," Eunice says as she steps out from behind the counter with a dust-cloth and walks stiffly toward a display cabinet. Walking has become more difficult for her in the past few weeks. You can almost hear her creak. Robert trails behind her.

"Hmm...same year that young fella from the choir went missing, wasn't it?" It's ridiculous, but even with no civilians in the room, Robert always uses the euphemistic "choir" instead of just coming out and saying "coven." His shiny bald head reflects the overhead lights, pulling Cat's attention like a beacon. If I could get enough launch power under me...

"Tom, you mean? Gillian's young man? I believe

it was."

"Wasn't there some rumor about you and..."

Eunice turns to him abruptly. I drop to a crouch, my back legs begging to spring. "Your point, Robert?"

"It's simply interesting that he disappeared, and then Cat showed up around the same time."

Eunice goes back to her dusting. "It's time to close for lunch. If you're not buying anything, you should move along."

He doesn't leave.

She turns back to him, a sharp edge to her words now. "Anything else you need? Anything?"

Robert shakes his head, ending the conversation. No one in Giles is brave enough to intentionally annoy Eunice except Gillian. As he nods, the lights shift enticingly from side to side on his glistening dome. I hunker down, ready to spring, but Eunice catches me with her eyes and gives me a fierce look that stops me before I can leap. I reluctantly settle in for a nap and tuck my face up under a leg so I can't be distracted by shiny things.

.

\*\*\*

After Robert leaves, Eunice picks me up and cradles me to her withered bosom. "I know you don't like him, Tom. But imagine if he knew you were spying on him all those years. Don't you think he'd kill you as soon as look at you? I know I would.

And you only have the nine lives. I won't have you lose another one so soon." And that's the problem. The old witch probably loves me in her own wicked, controlling way. And I'm dependent on her whacked-out love for everything I have. Still holding me close, she walks to the front door and flips the "Open" sign to "Closed" and locks up after checking the mailbox just outside the door. Her latest Archeology Today magazine has arrived, and I can see she's anxious to start paging through it. I've never known what she's looking for, but she always gets excited when a new one is delivered.

She heads toward the downstairs kitchenette, flipping through the pages in the digger's journal as she goes. "Will you behave today, Tom? If I fix you a nice lunch?"

I nod my adorable, tiny, kitten head and follow her to the kitchen.

"Good Tom," she says, absently.

I shift then, unexpectedly. I won't be eating out of my blue bowl after all. Once I'm oriented to my human limbs again, I walk upstairs to the bedroom and collect my red satin robe from the closet before I join her for our meal. At least she doesn't expect me to be naked every moment I spend in human form. No bare bottoms at the table, as Eunice says. She's all class, that one.

She also knows I'm easier to control if she lets me be a civilized human being for an hour or two every couple of days. Without that time, it's her own fault if Cat comes on strong even when I'm Tom. That she's letting me out already today tells me she has no intention of leaving me as Cat for too long, no matter how angry she was yesterday. She likes me as dependent as possible.

We dine on finger sandwiches and carrot sticks, as urbane as you please. She's quiet as she finishes skimming through her magazine. She makes a sour face as she closes it. Disappointed again. Maybe she's hoping they'll discover the body of someone she killed long ago and hid on an ancient magical site. It's just the kind of thing she'd love to gloat over.

She turns to me and comments on our latest visitor. "Every time Robert looks at me, I feel the wheels turning. Any minute, someone will arrive from the old folk's home with orders to take me. It's not enough that he controls the farmland on the north side of town, he wants my woodlands on the south as well. Probably thinks he'll control the coven if he controls the meeting grounds. And why was he asking about you after all these years, Tom?"

"Because he was in the car when Kevin ran me over."

"What's that?" Her eyes narrow to slits. Wrinkled, evil slits.

"I was going to tell you this morning, but you know I've never mastered Morse code by paw tap." Sometimes she enjoys my sarcasm. Other times, I'll find myself transformed and stuffed into my cage.

"He saw you after the death shift?"

"Kevin did. And if he described me—well, unlike someone uninitiated into 'our' world, Robert won't write it off as Kevin seeing things." It's wise not to tell her about the wink.

"This is very bad, Tom," she says, then inhales deeply when she realizes she's inadvertently issued a command. I shrink rapidly downward into the chair, growing fur. When the change is done, I pop my head back up over the edge of the table and use a paw to bring the last of my sandwich to my mouth. Although the question is now rhetorical because Cat can't answer, she exhales hard and asks harshly, "How could you let them see you?"

Like it matters. What do I care if people finally know what Eunice is capable of? What could she possibly do to me? She doesn't need to give me the snip: I'm already neutered.

I hop up onto the tabletop and lap at my tea while she rants.

***

Lunch hour is almost over when I hear a peck, peck, pecking at the door, "Yoo-hoo, Eunice, are you in there? Dad asked me to stop by about that interview."

Ugh. It's that smarmy wiggler, Kevin. As if having Dad around in the morning wasn't sufficient, now we've got Junior pushing his ugly face in. The only way he's an improvement is that he's still got just enough of a comb-over left that I won't be tempted by the full-on dome shine. Eunice's reaction isn't any kinder than mine. "Faugh! Now it's the son. I'll never be rid of them."

She has to go back out to the shop. Lunch hour is done, and we're open again for business. I follow her and retreat to a corner, but I'll be keeping an eye on him. The tip of my tail taps out a leisurely beat up, then down again, as I give him the full, unblinking evil eye through the door glass.

Natalie, local councilwomen and longstanding member of the "choir", is peering in the picture window to Kevin's side with her hand shading her eyes. Nat's shiny, red vinyl handbag hangs from her other arm. She'll be here for her "Magic Youth Masque", a Cat's Magical Shoppe specialty, mixed up fresh every week for any of the local residents willing to pay the price. Sometimes Eunice even sets me the task. The ingredients are simple enough, and Eunice only needs a second or two to add the magic. Natalie swears by it. She might not be so keen if she knew the main ingredient is finely grated fetal pig.

Eunice unlocks the door, ushering them in. As Nat walks by, she says, "Eunice, dear, you look nice today. Is that scarf new?"

"Just an old one I'd forgotten." Which, of course, she hadn't. Eunice never forgets. That works out well for holding grudges.

"It's nice all the same, dear. Is my treatment ready?"

"It's in the back. I'll get it. Kevin, you don't mind waiting." She doesn't bother to pretend it's a question, but Kevin does.

"No, no, Eunice. Plenty of time today. Take what you need." Kevin's public smile stays plastered on tight as he lurks toward the front of the store. He scans a pamphlet that touts seaweed as a restorative until she returns, packs up Natalie's treatment, and bids her goodbye, calling after her, "Don't forget to bring back the empty jars you still have at home, and I'll give a discount next week!"

As soon as the shop bell rings Natalie out, Kevin bustles to Eunice and hisses across the counter. "You said we'd talk."

"Keep your shirt on." Eunice counts the money in the till once, then counts it again. She's got to be doing it to annoy him. She can't have pulled in more than twenty bucks in cash so far today.

Kevin waits, his foot tapping restlessly on the ancient linoleum floor. Every so often, he gives me an appraising look that glides away before Eunice can catch him.

As choir members go, Robert's boy Kevin is a real wet rag. Other than an aptitude for potions, he has no particular skill with magic, and while he's shrewd, he's not who you'd want in your brain trust. Plus, his lumpy, doughy body doesn't give the ladies of the choir much to ogle at the now infrequent au naturel events. Not that the ladies in the Giles coven provide much of interest to leer at these days. Most are Gilly's age with Eunice, Robert, and Nat in the oldest contingent. Only a few of their children join in, and none of the grandchildren have stuck around Giles. It's not the kind of place where modern youngsters find their fun. They take off as quickly as they can and don't return. Like Eunice's Cassie, most of them have no knowledge of their hidden heritage.

Eunice walks to the shop door and flips the closed sign around again. Then she comes back and plucks me unceremoniously from my perch on the counter and plops me into the cage behind it. She beckons Kevin to follow with a twist of her head and heads for the kitchenette.

She *really* doesn't want me to know what they talk about.

*** 

Even with Cat's furry radar dishes tuned toward the hall, the conversation is too low for me to hear. I need out of here if I want to spy: fortunately, it's never been difficult to get out of the cage. The hard part is getting back in and getting the clip latched again so that Eunice doesn't know that I slipped my bonds.

Hmmm—maybe it's a little harder with kitten strength and smaller paws—nah, that's got it. The door flap hits the cage bars as it swings open it with a dull, aluminum clink. One graceful leap, and I'm out.

"Don't be stupid! A cat who becomes a man? Have you been dipping into your own potions?" Eunice's querulous voice lashes out as I slink toward the sound.

I hear Kevin's voice a moment later. "Whatever you deny or claim about your abilities, it was hard work keeping the cops out of that distasteful business at your cabins last summer. Do you know how much noble metal I poured into them to accomplish it? You said you'd pave the way for me to high priest."

Eunice stops him with a growl. "I said I would. But you put conditions on it. No death. No disability. It would be easier without having to be subtle."

"I never said subtle. I just said to get it done. But he's my father. I don't want him harmed, I just want the old man to step out of the way. Take a nice retirement."

Eunice says, "Then you'll have to give me time. Or do it yourself if you're so keen."

"If he figures out it's me maneuvering in the background, he'll disinherit me. No, thank you. And the side business you've got going from the shop? You promised me a partnership. And my little prize, Cassie? You've come through for me before, but you're holding out on me now."

"You have no idea the extent to which I've helped you! A worm like you…" I hear what sounds like a meaty palm hit the table, and Eunice barks, "Don't get physical, boy. You know I barely need to lift a finger to take you down. Be good and accept that I'll fulfill my promises in time."

Nothing happens for a moment, and I'm dying to know what's going on. Has she got him by the tongue again? Or by an even more delicate body part? I take the risk and poke my head around the doorway.

Well, that's boring. They're just sitting there glaring at each other. When Kevin looks away, Eunice says, "There. Much better. Do we need to have staring contests like children? No, I don't think so."

She stands and says, "Wait here. I've made something special for you to make up for our unfortunate spat the other night. If only your motives with me were as transparent as my gift to you."

I duck back in the hall, up against the wall, hoping she doesn't glance in my direction. She doesn't. Safe for now. I've got plenty of time before she makes it up the stairs and back down again.

I poke my head into the kitchen to see what Kevin is up to. He's holding a small glass vial full of brown liquid over Eunice's iced tea and watching its contents drain.

Well, this can't be good. What happens if she

drinks it? Mind control? Unconsciousness while he ransacks the house? Sexual imposition? Illness? Death? I wouldn't put any of those past him.

And then my heart stops beating as I realize: death. She could die. I'd be free. It starts beating again, wildly.

No. I can't think it. I can't.

I've wished her dead a hundred times, but when it comes down to it, I only want her dead in the abstract. I just want my freedom, my human life back. I wouldn't kill to get it. That would only prove my humanity is truly gone. I hear her footsteps again at the top of the stairs. I need to get back to the shop and my cage so I'm not found out and punished. But I also need to do something to keep Kevin from succeeding at his ghastly business. What I don't need is to keep crouching here paralyzed with indecision between the two alternatives.

Eunice steps into the hall and spots me where I still stand immobile. "Cat! How dare you defy me!"

She starts toward me, dropping the brown-paper-wrapped package she carries. Kevin's gift hits the tile below with a whunk. When she reaches the kitchen door, I dart through, my decision made.

She nearly has my tail, but I leap away onto the chair, then up to the table, and careen into the glass, bowling it over, spilling the tea with its mysterious payload to flow onto the floor in a brown waterfall. The glass spins off the edge of the table and shatters when it hits the floor, shards spraying in all directions. Eunice reaches out and backhands me so that I go spinning off the edge of the table, too. I'm hurt, but I don't shatter.

A splinter of glass slices a back paw when I land, but I run away on three legs, favoring the fourth. I bolt for my cage, pull the door shut behind me, and manipulate the latch back into place. A trail my blood leads from the cage to the hall. Eunice steps into the shop, sees I'm back where I belong, and returns to the kitchen.

A moment later, she re-enters the shop with Kevin in lock step behind her. He's carrying the package she dropped earlier. If his eyes were swords, he'd have sliced me into single-size servings of cat as he passed.

Eunice sees him out and reopens the shop for business.

She leans under the counter, and I gaze up at her with Cat's most sincere look of contrition. All I get for saving her life is a snort.

I clean my sore paw, tasting blood and tea.

I WAKE IN THE DARK, confused how I could have slept so long. My head feels as furry on the inside as it does on the outside. Then I realize I must have taken in some of Kevin's potion when cleaning my paws. A wet paw is an annoyance no cat can ignore. At least the potion didn't kill me.

My cage door is open now. Eunice must have relented and opened it while I slept. I check the windows, but they're closed tight. I'm sure she's still angry with me for dying so publicly and drawing attention to powers she doesn't want anyone to know she has. I can't go out so I can prowl and play. That's my punishment. Locked up for the night.

My sore paw feels better after my long sleep, and I'm restless. I go searching for something to do. I find a spool of ribbon on the counter downstairs that Eunice used to pretty up Natalie's Magic

Masque.

The spool hits the floor with a thwack and then rolls. I bat at it tentatively, and it goes spinning along, but the ribbon isn't unreeling the way I want it to. I give it the once-over and manage to locate the problem. I grab on to the sides of the spool with sharp little claws and then tug at the end of the tucked-in ribbon with my teeth. Problem solved.

With one bat of a paw, the spool is traveling across the floor with the ribbon spiraling out behind it as it goes. So I leap, and I jump, and I roll, and I tangle. And then I give it another bat in the opposite direction and repeat. If a cat could laugh, I'd be giggling my head off.

Did I say that sometimes it's not so bad being Cat? Because it's true. I don't have to drudge away at a soul-killing job. And the Goddess knows I get plenty of sleep.

On the other hand, the world doesn't look as good through a cat's eyes. The reds are missing: peppers, lady bugs, roses, fire trucks—they all fade to gray. I'd mourn the loss, but then I catch a tiny grain of movement that could be dinner, and I'm off to chase a beetle.

After I've wrung as much fun out of the ribbon as I can, I'm off exploring in the kitchenette, trailing the spool of ribbon behind me because a piece of it is caught in a back claw, and I can't be bothered to spend the time untangling it.

There are a few interesting-smelling bits of food

trapped in the drain strainer. I end up spitting them back out, though, because they don't taste anywhere near as good as they smell.

I've probably killed an hour now, and I've poked my head into as many intriguing corners as I can find, but I'm not able to scare up any other fun, so I navigate some nesting circles preparatory to settling in for a nap. When a car backfires in front of the shop, I leap straight up in the air, my bright green ribbon streamer traveling with me. I'm ashamed for being such a scaredy-cat, but I'm young again now, and Cat's instincts will need to refine themselves before I stop jumping at noises.

Alert again, I head for the bedroom. If the backfire woke Eunice up and she's in a better mood, she could dangle the ribbon for me to chase, or she'd pet me for a while before we settle back in to sleep. I sit in the bedside chair and give her the slow-blink stare, but she doesn't sense me and respond. I launch myself onto the bed and scramble over her, going back and forth for a while trying to get her attention, then I finally settle into a hollow in the bedspread to sleep. The ribbon, which had no choice but to follow me in my rambles across her body, wraps her up like a gift.

I hate Eunice for holding me captive all these years; I really do. But I'm so lonely. And Cat never could hold a grudge. He just wants to play.

It's chilly when I wake again. Usually, Eunice puts out more than enough heat for both of us. The sun is blazing through the window now, well above the horizon, and I rub my head against her back one more time, purring loudly, but she doesn't roll over and stroke me like she usually does.

I try again. No response. I get distracted briefly by the ribbon still caught on a back claw and finally take the time to disentangle it with my teeth.

I make one more trip across her body, traveling the path of the ribbon, and look her in the face. Her lips are faintly blue. Her eyes are open wide and staring.

It takes a minute for me to realize that she's gone, that I'd wrapped my own present last night and awakened to a surprise party.

Ding dong, the witch is dead. It finally happened. I'm free of her. Eunice, my lover, my jailor, is gone.

It takes another minute for me to realize that I'm really all alone in the world now, that I'm still Cat, the windows are sealed, and I've got no way to hunt or to open a tin of food for breakfast. Suddenly, my new freedom doesn't feel all that free.

\*\*\*

I sit in the bedside chair for a long while, forcing Cat to stay focused so that I can think. If only I hadn't talked back to Eunice two nights ago, I'd still be the mature Cat, and the windows would be wide open so that I could roam at night. I could easily take care of myself by hunting. It wouldn't be ideal. I still wouldn't be human like I'd hoped would happen when she died, but at least I could save Cat from an empty belly.

And then it hits me—Cat with an empty belly. How long will it be before Eunice starts to smell like food? I have to get out of here. Now.

I focus Cat the best I can and systematically explore every possible means of escape, but there's no way out. I try to topple one of the big glass lamps into a window to break it, but my attempts to capsize it accomplish nothing except a sore spot on the top of the head. The lamp barely wobbles.

I scour both kitchens for any hint of food—nothing. Not one scrap except the drain bits I rejected yesterday. Cat has always been a great mouser, so there isn't a single furry pest left anywhere within these walls.

The phone rings unexpectedly, and my hackles rise until Cat registers that the sound is harmless. Cassie's voice comes out of the speaker after the message plays. "Granny, is your cell off again? Just call me when you get this. Dan came and got his things, although I couldn't leave them out on the lawn and ended up bringing them back in again. You'd be proud of me, though. I didn't break down and apologize for the pants. So, anyway, call me."

Sorry, Cassie, Eunice doesn't live here any more. And the only inhabitant of the house doesn't have an opposable thumb or the right vocal setup necessary to pick up the receiver and let you know that.

The best I can hope for is that someone will be curious when the shop doesn't open for business Tuesday morning. But that still means I have to make it through tonight, tomorrow, and tomorrow night on my own. All that time with Eunice beginning to smell more and more delicious.

I find a dark spot as far away from the tempting smell coming down the stairwell as I can and pull my head into my chest as I make myself comfortable for a long day of napping uninterrupted by food. I try not to think about the meal waiting for me upstairs, all wrapped up in a nice green ribbon.

I spend the rest of the day in the showcase window out front when I'm not napping, but the passersby are used to seeing Cat there and think nothing of it. Some of them stop to coo at me and remark on Eunice's new kitten, but apparently none of them possess powers of ESP because I'm thinking extremely choice thoughts at all of them, particularly the kitten-cooers. If they have to be that sickeningly precious, they could at least read my mind and get me something to eat.

Around sunset, I begin to slam myself against the window every time someone walks by. Right now, there's a pair of teens canoodling as they walk past on the street. Come on, get your hands off each other and look at me!

And then, beyond them and across the street, the glint of streetlight on a bald pate flashes and catches my attention.

Kevin is leaning up against the brick facade of the bakery. He looks me right in the eye and smirks. I see it in his face—he knows Eunice has left the building. But how could he? I broke the glass he put the potion in, and I took my smack for it. He saw me do it just before she hustled him out.

And that's when I slept my drugged sleep and woke up after Eunice had gone to bed.

Had he come back? Done something I didn't see? Did he have something to do with Eunice's death? Why else would he be standing there gloating at me from across the street? I can almost hear him thinking *that's right, buddy. See what being the favorite gets you?*

IN THE MORNING, I hold one paw up so that the drip from the bathtub faucet splashes on to the back. Then I hustle to lap it up before the precious droplet runs off and away. It takes half the day to get a decent drink and slake my thirst. Plus, the hunger's getting worse, and it's only been a day and a half since I woke up next to Eunice's cold body.

The smell is enticing after an additional day to let her juices stew. Cat fights me every second as I resist his instinct not to let meat go to waste. I stay by the glass, meowing piteously whenever someone walks by, trying to let them know I need help. But they just walk on, remarking on the cuteness of Eunice's new kitten.

The phone rings for the sixth time in two days: it's Cassie again, leaving another message, each of them increasingly concerned in tone after Granny doesn't respond to the whimpers about her broken heart. This call's even a little frantic.

Finally, I knock the handset to the floor and do my best crying-baby imitation, a sound passed genetically from cat to cat to control their humans. The crying combined with the phone that will never be placed back on the hook should get some action. She'll be forced to investigate why Granny isn't answering. I hear the click on the other end of the line and picture her running to her car and speeding toward Giles from Boston, throwing everything else aside in concern for her granny's cat. Okay, not for me, maybe, but for her granny, yes.

I think about rescuing the ribbon from Eunice's room to entertain myself until my call for help bears fruit, but then I think better of it. If I get too close, Cat is almost sure to decide the Eunice-steaks upstairs shouldn't be left to age any longer.

So, I'll wreak kitteny havoc to keep his mind off it. What to do in defiance that I would have loved to do when witchy-poo was still alive? My eyes drift around the shop. There it is—the perfect rebellion.

Eunice had a thing for anything Egyptian. She put an entire cemetery's worth of canopic burial jars around the top of the shop a few years ago. In ancient Egypt, they held the internal organs of mummies, but in Giles, they're popular for holding the ashes of the town's beloved pets.

The jar right above the door, the one decorated as a stylized black cat? She always threatened it would be my final resting place if I caused her too much grief. I'd love to send it crashing to the floor and watch it shatter, sending shards of painted clay scattering everywhere. I deserve a celebration for outliving her.

But no matter how I puzzle it out, there's no way for me to get up there. The jars are too close to the ceiling on their specially built ledges, and there's nothing I can use to climb up.

Instead, I maneuver to the top shelf of the potions case through a series of jumps and restarts, which Eunice would never have allowed. I'd have gotten the business end of a broom if she even knew I'd been thinking about it. The bottles are packed together tightly in their ordered rows, but there's just enough room behind them that I can squeeze in and push through the canyon created between the bottles and the shelf. There's a satisfying crash or two as I work my way along, but the majority of the bottles survive my trek. Maybe I'll get lucky and the ones that fell will have something in them worth eating.

When I reach the other side, I try for the top shelf across the aisle, but I misjudge and can only slow myself a little with my claws scrabbling at each of the shelves as I fall. It's not too bad when I hit— I'm still young and flexible. I'm recovering my dignity, shaking my paws ferociously—they're soaked with something that smells suspiciously like cannabis—when I hear a voice sound faintly through the door, "Oh, you poor thing."

It's Gillian, peering in at me. Why would she be here? The shop doesn't open today. Oh! It was me—I did it. Clever me. Cassie must have called her. I knew I'd get someone's attention if I kept at it.

She knocks on the door with a loud rap-tap, and when no one comes to answer, she rings the bell. I sit still and composed, watching her with as somber a face as I can manage given what Cat has to work with.

Gillian tries the door handle, but it doesn't move. I spring into action, running to the door, leaping upward to the old-fashioned turn-latch on the inside to let her in, but I can't budge it, and Gilly doesn't really need my help. If she wants in, she'll be in.

With her hand still on the handle, she closes her eyes, concentrating. I hear the click of tumblers moving on their own. She twists the handle and enters the shop but stops abruptly when she raises her hand to cover her nose and mouth, then comes to me and scoops me up.

"Oh, my Goddess...the smell! Come on. Let's get you out of here." She carries me outside, leaving the shop door wide open.

Gilly fumbles her cell phone out of her bag one-handed and dials three digits. The police are quick to respond. Not surprising, since most of them spend all their time in the café down the street guzzling endless cups of coffee with Kevin while he pretends to be a newsman. I'd seen him slip doses of a light-blue potion with coppery flecks into their cups when they weren't looking, a fact I dutifully reported back to Eunice. She smiled and kept her reasons to herself. More of their blasted secrets.

Gillian strokes me behind the ears and cuddles me against her shoulder as she waits on the various officials to complete their jobs. "I never liked her much, but it's still sad when someone dies alone like that."

Gillian was always kind. I was such a fool to be led astray so long ago. I rub the side of my head against her chin, marking her as mine. Maybe, if I can't be human again, she'll take me in, and I can live out my last three Cat lives with her. It's the second best thing I can think of having happen.

After Eunice's remains are carried down in a body bag and stowed in the mortuary van, Gilly goes back into the shop, still snugging me close with one hand. She walks around the counter to find my cage and moves it onto the counter top, then gently sets me inside. "Now, let's get the windows open." She gives me one last chuck under the chin, and I lick her hand furiously, hoping she'll get the hint. She laughs. No, she doesn't get it. I give her a gentle bite. "Ouch! You little scamp! I've got a couple more calls to make, but first, maybe I should find you something to eat."

Holding the phone against her shoulder with her cheek while her busy hands scoop out food into a dish, she pages through the phone book and finds a specialty service for emergency cleanup. She agrees to stay until the service arrives, her demeanor totally business while she describes the situation. A bed and a smell to be removed, she says. It's growing dark as she calls Cassie, her voice at its most soothing.

"Cass? It's Gillian. I'm at the house now like you asked, and I have very bad news about your grandmother."

I don't hear the rest of the call. I'm purring madly with my face shoved gratefully into a dish of fishily fragrant wet food that masks the lingering, sweetish smell of death.

***

I was bummed out after Gilly left that night. That's what? Two days ago now. I'd hoped she'd take me with her, but she made her excuses sweetly, saying, "I'm sorry, Cat, but I have to leave you here. I have my Polly, and she's too old now to try to adapt her ways to having a cat around. I think one or the other of you would end up in a bad way."

I'd forgotten about Polly, my cockatoo. Man, she'd cared for her all these years? I suppose I should have known she wouldn't just abandon her. But she was right: Polly would dispose of Cat easily. He'd never have a chance against that beak.

Gilly comes in the morning to feed me my wet food and set out a bowl of the hard stuff for later in the day, but she doesn't stay long. Why would she? I'm her rival's cat, as far as she knows. She loves me up and talks to me, but I'm less attentive to what she has to say. I'm going feral and Cat is taking over. Gillian's words are nowhere near as interesting as smells and patterns and the birdsong coming in through the windows.

Cat spends hours trying to compact himself small enough to get out through the two-inch high crack in the back window so he can run to the woods to hunt. After a while, he catches on that he's never going to get through and takes a nap. But then he's right back at it afterwards. He's forgotten what he learned about the solidity of his own head the first time. And I've forgotten, too.

It's starting: I'm beginning to lose my human, thinking half.

"GILLY FILLED ME IN on the new Cat, but I didn't think you'd be such a tiny thing." Cassie lets the door swing shut and sets her suitcase on the floor as she reaches out a hand to me. Cat sniffs it before he'll let her touch him. He's losing his domestic habits, so I hope Cassie is here to stay. I don't know if it will work for someone other than Eunice, but I need to find a way to get her to say those two little words, "good Tom," and I need to do it quick.

"It's so quiet without customers or Granny." Her voice breaks. She stops scratching my ears and picks up her case again. She walks up the stairs, and I trail behind her. Cat wants to rub against her ankles, get her attention back, but I fight him with every ounce of control I've got. The last thing I need is for Cassie to trip over me and end up at the bottom of the stairs with a broken neck. That wouldn't help me out, that's for sure.

A few years ago, Cassie was a sweet but naive teenager who Eunice ordered around like a navvy. I always wished she'd get a little spunk although I couldn't help feeling a little protective of her. And, oh, the angst that can pour out of a teenage girl to a cat who's willing to listen in exchange for chin-scratching, ear rubs, and long, sensual strokes along the length of his back.

But when Cassie was around for the summer, I didn't get to spend much time in human form. How would Eunice have explained me? I was stuck with the bare minimum time when Cassie was out for softball practice or seeing a friend. I admit I sometimes resented her a little. But if she's my only shot to make it back to humanity instead of losing myself forever to Cat, I'll do anything to keep her safe.

She stands for a while, peering into Eunice's red-draped bedroom. The bed is gone now, taken by the cleaners, but the rest of the room still looks like a cross between a Victorian sitting room and a seventies sex-palace. Through Cat's eyes, the room is furnished in dull grays, but the reds are there for me when I'm human. They were a nice change of pace when I came back from being Cat. She'd planned it one weekend when she was especially pleased with me. Unlike most of the gifts she gave me, she never took that one back.

As Cassie stands there looking in to her grandmother's chamber of libidinous, she begins to cry, the tears rolling silently down her cheeks. When her nose starts to run, she moves on to the room at the end of the hall that was always hers when she stayed with us.

She sits on the edge of the bed, opening her purse and pulling out a small packet of tissues, which she uses to blow her nose delicately. Afterward, she dries her eyes with a long sweep along her sleeve.

"Well, Cat, it seems there's no place for me to be now that isn't full of sadness. I don't want to live in Boston any more, but I don't want this house without Granny in it, either. Moving to Giles and taking over the shop is what she wanted for me, but it doesn't feel right. I half-expected her to be here, playing some awful joke on me."

The suggestion alarms me, but I push away the fear. Cat was primed to have Eunice for dinner. Even she couldn't be that good at faking dead.

Cassie flops back on the bed and stares up at the ceiling, completely still except for the tears that flow into her hair as she starts crying again. I jump up on the bed and crawl between her small, soft breasts. She lays a hand across my back and pets me gently, talking quietly.

"In just one week, I've lost three people I love. Not just Granny, but Dan—I thought I'd be with him forever. And Charlie, my best friend, too. When I asked her how she could have gone to bed with Dan, she said they'd never even been attracted to each other! But she suddenly just wanted to see him, and when Dan opened the door, they fell into each other's arms without even speaking—I can't believe my best friend and the man I love would do that."

Ha! There's a clue to what Eunice meant when she'd said it was sorted. She must have worked a spell on Cassie's loved ones to get what she wanted. Too bad for Eunice she'd catapulted into the great beyond instead of being here to greet Cassie when she arrived.

I frisk away to the window, then come back to her and do a little leap / twirl combo, then run back to the window, pushing my nose into the seam where the fresh air comes in, repeating the attempt to get her attention until even cat tires of it. She's not going to catch on and open the window so that I can get out to hunt. In fact, I don't think she knows I'm in the room. I leave the girl to continue her staring contest with the ceiling fan while I prowl the shadows for the rest of the night.

Just before the sun rises, I make my way back to the bedroom and jump up on the bed to settle in for my morning nap. She's still lying there, staring at the ceiling, wearing the same clothes.

We're quite a pair: a cat and a catatonic. At least Eunice left Cassie her humanity when she destroyed her life.

\*\*\*

Cassie finally turns on her side and her breathing slows to the regular rhythm that marks sleep. Her hair splays out and cascades off the side of the bed. I go off the bed behind it to bat lazily at the silky dark brown strands where they lay loose and inviting.

Then, a glint of light flashes off the buckle of her suitcase as the rising sun peeks through the window, and I make a leap to capture it. I catch it, then lift my paw, but the glint is gone. I withdraw and try to figure out where the silver went, and it's back again. I pounce, lift my paw, and again, it's gone. I withdraw and try to figure out where the silver went.

I finally stop myself after ten or so repeat performances. I'm beginning to think like a cat full time. I have to shift human soon if I'm going to save myself and be a man again. I hope it works if I get Cassie to say the words. Even though she doesn't know she's practiced magic, she's a witch the same as her grandmother. Eunice secretly had her working spells to test her abilities. Cassie never caught on that the "calming chants" and "sending warm thoughts rituals" were actually incantations Eunice had her combine with the shop's ingredients.

I know it's a stretch, but Eunice was careful to never call me by my real name in front of others, and if she slipped, she'd immediately remark on me being a "tomcat" to cover it up. There are only two possible reasons she'd have kept my name a secret: she worried that someone would guess what happened to Tom Sanders, or another person who knew my name could reveal me with the same combination of words. I'm hoping for the latter.

I pad through the house, focusing Cat as much as I can, while I take inventory of objects that might be useful.

There's a ball point pen under the couch, but I lack the ability to manipulate it. I once spent two days trying to write Gilly a note by holding a pen in my mouth. It didn't work. No matter how hard I tried, I could only make random marks that didn't approach penmanship. Eunice eventually found my hidden stack of paper and had a good laugh.

I also know from experience that no matter how adept I think I am at shaping words from meows, no one understands a single one but me. What else is there?

The Ouija boards! If Cassie suddenly gets the urge to avail herself of the Ouija boards from the shop to talk to granny one more time, I could push a planchette to spell a message. But she's always been a sensible girl, unlikely to turn to the occult for solace. And the heavy wooden spirit boards are stacked on top of each other on an upper shelf in the corner of the shop. Eunice moved them off the counter years ago to a place I couldn't reach. She was always a step ahead of me.

There must be something. Anything. How can I

give Cassie a message if I can't talk and I don't have the dexterity for writing? What can I use, if I can't use the Ouija?

I peruse my paws where they meet the linoleum and it hits me. Oh, how simple. Why not use the floor? It's a perfect writing surface if a cat is clever, and I'm the cleverest cat in this town, hands down. But what can I use for ink? If I start breaking jars, I'll get caught before I'm done. So that's out. Wait—I have the perfect idea.

Behind the counter, the trash can beckons. I leap to the rim and hang there for a moment before it topples over onto me. I twist away, scrambling out from underneath to view the result. The plastic can didn't make much noise when it bounced against the linoleum. I think I've gone undetected.

I go to work: a banana peel goes here, crumpled receipts there, a used tissue below them, and a yogurt cup there. I run out of trash when it just says "goo." No good.

I think again, reviewing my resources. Then, I systematically raid the bins, pushing packets of herbs into rows to continue forming letters. It's not enough, though. I've got "good t" but that won't do it. I raid higher up the shelves and bring back tapered candles one by one in my mouth. My teeth and claws are covered with wax by the time I'm done. But it's there: good tom. Every letter. I jump up on the counter and admire my handiwork. When she walks into the room, she'll read it and say it, and I'll be freed. I jump off the counter and go to the far side of the message so that she has to see it when she finds me.

Time for my nap. My last one as a cat?

\*\*\*

"Cat, are you hungry?" Cassie calls from the kitchenette.

Yes! Yes! Yes! I spring awake and am off like a shot until I remember—no, she has to come find me. She has to come find *them*, the words, the magical words. I sit in front of the shop door, surveying my handiwork again and finding it good. I face the doorway she's got to come through and start bleating so she'll know where to find me.

Minutes pass. "Cat? Are you coming?"

No, no I'm not. You come to me. I bleat louder.

"Cat, stop that terrible noise and come get your num-nums."

Num-nums? Really? At least she's moving now. In a minute, she'll see what I've done, read the words out, and then I'll be bursting out of my cat body, triumphant.

Maybe. At least I'll know whether the words work for someone other than Eunice. If I had fingers, every single one of them would be crossed.

I wait for it. I wait for it. I wait for it. And there she is, stepping through the doorway and around the counter, eyes meeting mine, ready to look down, see the words, say the words. But before she does, her foot slides as she puts it down on one of the extra candles I'd abandoned when I didn't need it. It slips beneath her foot, taking her leg out at an awkward angle and puts her off balance.

She bobbles backward and flings her arms out to steady herself. She manages to push off from the counter before she knocks her head against it and ends up moving too swiftly in the other direction, falling forward now with arms outstretched.

She lands helter-skelter in the center of my hard work, her splayed limbs shoving the carefully placed objects out of their spots until it's just a pile of trash again with no meaning.

She sits up, rubbing her elbow, then her knee, surveying the mess. She seems okay. Nothing broken.

"Cat? What the?"

I slink to the kitchenette.

No point in lingering at the place of my defeat.

Cassie's moved the tidy stack of journals off the table and onto the counter. I'd throw them away if it was me. It's not like Eunice is going to come along and scold her for getting rid of them. And my bowl doesn't belong on the floor, either. I'm not used to eating alone. Cassie knows I've always eaten at the table. She needs to learn the drill.

As Cassie walks into the kitchenette, still rubbing an elbow and grimacing, I jump up onto the table where she's laid out her own plate and silverware. I turn my gaze toward the bowl on the ground below and then back to her again.

"Bad Cat! What's gotten into you? It's going to take me forever to clean up the mess in the shop. And you've ruined most of the candles." She picks me up and sets me on the floor next to the bowl. I jump up onto the table again, and once again, she says, "Bad Cat!" and moves me to the floor.

I jump back up on the table, and before she has time to react, I leap to the floor, where I look up for her response. She's smiling.

"Oh, good Cat!"

Hmmm…okay, new plan. Maybe a more subtle form of manipulation will set me free.

I've always thought that the power of the curse resides in my collar. Then again, what do I know? I was only playing at being a warlock—Gillian was the witch in the family. I've had around forty-five years now to try to scrape it off, slip out of it, cut through it, and…nothing.

But I discovered early on in my captivity that my name is written on the inside. The lettering is faint and written in Eunice's tidy script. The rusty color of the ink makes me think it might be blood. Mine, even. Although the collar won't turn fully inside out, it twists on its side with enough space between my neck and the leather that someone looking for it might make the writing out clearly. If I can find a way to make Cassie read it, then maybe I can get her to start calling me by my name. After that, I just         have to be very, very, very good.

ALL DAY LONG, I scratch and dig at the collar whenever Cassie glances at me. My neck is sore from the extra attention. It's does me no good. She doesn't catch on. You'd almost think I'm not the focus of her universe. Eunice would have noticed.

I watch her go through her day, sometimes weepy, sometimes wearing a sappy, nostalgic expression as she clears out a drawer and finds an old photo or a playbill for a local summer theater.

I've never seen grief like this before. Eunice didn't shed a tear for any of the supposed friends she lost through her many years. The only time I ever saw her cry was when her first gray hair appeared.

Cassie is different. She's soft and kind like Gillian. No wonder I always thought she was dull— she has the same qualities of niceness and forgiveness that made me believe it would be okay to sneak around on Gillian for a splash of excitement. I used to think womanizing was just part of being a man. I know now it wasn't. If I could choose again, I'd take loving and kind over excitement any day. No one knows better than I do where too much excitement lands you.

She places a batch of papers on the desk, and I jump up to plant myself firmly in the middle of the stack. I start worrying the collar with a paw, but she ignores me after she pushes me off to the side and continues reading. In a few minutes, I creep toward her stack of papers again, but she picks me up almost roughly, saying, "I've had enough of that! You're going to need to learn how to behave," and marches with me to my cage, where she plops me unceremoniously inside and then walks back up the stairs to the study, leaving me alone.

I have to say, that came from left field. Not at all what I was expecting.

At dinner time, she lets me out, and I follow her into the kitchenette, chastened by my time alone. As she's setting my bowl down, I give one more half-hearted scratch at the collar, and she finally gets a clue.

"You've been picking at that collar all day, Cat Is there something poking you? Is it too tight?" There, that's what I was expecting from such a sweet and well-behaved girl who has always been concerned with the welfare of others. She picks me up and holds me in her lap, running her fingers around the inside of the collar. "It feels loose enough, and there's nothing sharp on the inside." She examines it more closely, trying to undo the buckle, which I know from experience can't be undone. "That buckle is frozen in place, isn't it? It's like it's fused. It's not coming off that way."

She runs a finger under the collar again and pulls it away from my neck to examine it more closely. I hold my breath in anticipation until she says, "It says 'Tom' in here. Is that your name? Tom?"

I purr up a storm. I rub against her like a madcat. I am one feline love machine.

Cassie laughs a weak little laugh. "Well, even if it's not, I guess you like it. Might as well be Tom from here on in. 'Cat' has always been too generic for my tastes, and you're my cat now, I guess, not Gran's."

Of course, that just sets her off crying again. It may be a while before I can get her to notice what a good Tom I am.

*** 

I hear the sobs starting to form in Cassie's voice as she talks into the phone, "But Daddy, I held the funeral off this long hoping that you and Jan would change your minds and come. I know you had a terrible relationship with her, but she was your mother."

A male voice responds, but I can't hear what he

says.

"Fine. Be that way. Maybe you hate her, but you could be here for *me*!" Cassie flings the phone into the couch, where it lands with a whump.

I hear knocking and rush to the front of the shop to investigate. Cassie trails behind me slowly, laboring to get herself under control as she wipes away her tears.

Gilly waves at Cassie through the glass. Behind her, most of the female members of the coven stand in line with covered dishes and baked goods.

Cassie opens the door, protesting weakly, "You guys shouldn't have."

"We wanted to, sweetie. We know how much work it's going to be to sort out your grandmother's personal affairs, not to mention the house and shop." Gilly sets her basket on the shop counter and pulls Cassie in for a huge hug, rubbing her back to comfort her. "Plus, you'll need to feed people at the wake, so it's not all for you. Now, some of this will need to be refrigerated." Gilly lets her go. Cassie seems calmer now. "Do you want it in the kitchenette or the kitchen upstairs?"

"The kitchenette, I guess. I hadn't even thought about food. Even though I made the arrangements, it's so hard to keep remembering that she's gone." Cassie starts to mist up, and Gillian engulfs her again.

"There, there, sweetheart, you're such a good girl. Your grandmother was so lucky to have you."

From the back of the pack, I hear Natalie add under her breath, "With her poison personality, she was lucky to have anyone." Some of the others must have heard her, too, because they cough quietly to hide their titters.

"Come on, girls, let's get this stowed away in the back." Gillian leads the way, and the other food-bearers follow. I stay well out of the way of all those tramping feet.

Cassie and Gillian say goodbye at the shop door only a few minutes later, and Gillian adds, "Don't hesitate to call me if you need anything at all," as she releases her from a final hug.

Just as Cassie starts to lock up shop again, Kevin yoo-hoos as he bustles along the sidewalk from the café, heading toward her.

She waits as Kevin comes rushing up. He thrusts his hand out for her to shake, which she does, but with little enthusiasm.

"It's been years since I watched you play softball, but I always enjoyed cheering your team on. My father was a great friend of your grandmother—he's Robert Andrews, head of the town council?"

"Yeah, I remember you, Kevin. The shop isn't open yet." What I remember is she and her teammates used to giggle and make vomiting sounds on the phone about "Kreepy Kevin." He doesn't have children. He just gets off on watching teenage girls.

"Oh no, no. I don't need anything from the

shop. I just wanted to tell you how sorry I am about your grandmother. Eunice was important to the town. I interviewed her for an article about the store just the other day...I noticed you said "yet" about keeping the shop open. You're continuing with it, then?"

"I don't know. I'll at least be giving it a trial run as long as I'm here. I can't say in the long term."

"Oh sure, sure. I understand." He leans in closer, his eyes darting down to her breasts as he does, and they linger there before returning to her face. "If there's anything at all I can do to help you or make you feel more comfortable here, please don't hesitate to call me." He offers her his card. "I'm available any time, day or night."

He dawdles too long before he lets go of the business card, which she places in the back pocket of her nicely filled-out jeans, and his voice takes on a low, intimate tone. Enough of that.

I have his ankle before he has time to fend it off, and I get in a good chomp through his thin dress sock. He bursts out with, "Damn that cat," as he looks down. Cassie looks down, too.

"Bad Tom!" Cassie blurts out before he shakes me off forcefully and sends me sliding across the fresh-waxed floor.

She runs after me and grabs me up to the bosom Kevin has no business admiring. She strokes me soothingly as she turns back to him, "You didn't have to be so harsh. He's just a kitten!"

Kevin doesn't quite have himself back under control yet. "Oh yes, *just* a kitten." He looks switchblades at me. "He started it." He lifts his pant leg and shoves his sock around his ankle to reveal four small drops of blood oozing from the bite. "Got a good one in, too." His public face takes over again before he says, "But I'm sorry I reacted so strongly."

Cassie's anger recedes as her natural concern for others kicks in. "I had no idea. Sorry I yelled. He can be a little pest. I'm sorry he hurt you, but you have to admit he's adorable."

"Oh yes, adorable," he says, but his expression is predatory. I've been a cat for a long time, a predator myself. I've known what he is since I flew across the table to break that glass. I'll be keeping two watchful eyes on him for Cassie's sake.

CASSIE HAS BEEN A BLUBBERING MESS since she got up this morning. When Gilly appears in the doorway of the back parlor that leads to the shop, her face overflowing with loving concern, I'm more than glad she's here. Cat is fascinated by the swirling fabric of her flowing black skirt, but I use all the focus I have left to keep him from going after it. I bound onto the couch and coil into a ball to keep myself under control. She tells Cassie, "The sign is up on the door to come around to the back now, and I've shut and locked the door into the shop. The last thing you need is Giles' less refined residents making off with your stock in Eunice's memory."

Cassie thanks her as she loads one of Eunice's silver trays with a selection of finger foods and then places it back in the fridge. "I'm ready, I guess. As ready as I can be."

She looks sophisticated with her hair tucked up into a neat bun, and she's attired elegantly in a simple black dress. How is it that I never noticed how pretty she is? Eunice was strikingly beautiful when she was young, and Cassie doesn't have a patch on that, but there's something about Cassie that is definitely her own. I see it now. I don't know why I haven't before.

"Come on then, let's go say goodbye, pet. I know it's overwhelming right at the moment, but a good funeral does a lot to get the healing started." Gillian hands Cassie the small black purse that matches her funeral attire and takes her arm. I like seeing them together like this. Cassie got the wrong grandmother.

They're on their way then, but Cassie stops, comes back, and gives me a quick scratch behind the ears just before they head out the back door. "Tom, you be a good boy while I'm gone." Gilly's back stiffens just the slightest at my name. She turns to stare at me, then shakes her head and rolls her eyes, smiling quietly to herself.

Phew! If Cassie had put those words in a slightly different order, things would have gotten freaky fast. There'd be more than a quizzical look and the shaking off of what Gilly must believe is a silly thought. I can't make my first human contact with Cassie with my ex-wife as a witness. I'd have too much explaining to do. What could I say after all these years? Sorry wouldn't even scrape the surface.

***

In November, 1967, Eunice was a young man's ideal Mrs. Robinson with her white gloves, petite hat, and fitted Jackie Onassis suits. I know she wasn't hip, but she was one foxy older woman. And Gilly had started pressuring me to let her stop taking The Pill and start making babies. I just wasn't ready for the family trip. I was only twenty-one.

The affair was a blast at first. Eunice was newly divorced and knew things that none of my previous partners had a clue about. She was a true advertisement for the charms of an "experienced woman." But after a while, I didn't like being treated like a toy Eunice could set on a shelf until she wanted me. She was dating Robert by then. I don't think she had any feelings for him, but he was beginning to build power within the city government and that appealed to her. She made it clear she wanted to continue what we were doing, but we couldn't be public, at least not right away. I guess she assumed I'd want to leave Gillian for her after I'd tasted her charms.

I think Gilly knew, but she never said anything. What could she do? Ask for a divorce? Times were different. Women had a hard time on their own. I knew she'd stick it out with me. And I knew she loved me. I finally made the decision to tell Eunice it was over, but I ended up a cat anyway. I don't know how it happened. I woke up after our one-last-time-for-old-time's-sake, and everything had changed.

"Write it, Tom," Eunice said, handing me the pen and a sheet of paper with a Boston hotel's watermark. I refused.

"Come on, Eunice, don't be a drag. It was fun, but now it's over...so wave your magic wand and let me get back to my wife."

"Don't be bad, Tom."

The first time I shifted, I thought I was having a nightmare. I was sure I'd wake up and be back to normal when it passed. I had no idea how important those words would become to my life.

We went back and forth for most of an afternoon. I thought she'd tire of it—bad Tom, good Tom—as I was first a cat, then a man, then cat, then man again. The change was horribly painful those first few days. It's not much better now. I'm just used to it.

After she kept Cat in a cage for two days without food and water, I caved in. I wrote what she wanted me to write, the letter that told Gilly I'd had an affair with Eunice, that I'd left because Eunice had thrown me over and I couldn't bear life without her.

It must have been convincing. Gilly never accused Eunice of anything more than driving me away.

***

I have no time to waste. Although Eunice's funeral is today, I can't sit mourning for her, even if I was sure I'd want to.

How can I leave Cassie another message, one that can't injure her? I take a tour of the upstairs—it has to be up here, because the downstairs will soon be inhabited by the Giles "choir" and assorted hangers-on. The message I need to leave has to be somewhere private that only Cassie will see.

No one would go into Eunice's room even if they do venture up the stairs to avail themselves of the upstairs bathroom. I'll have privacy for my efforts if I keep them in there. And I have just the thing.

I jump to Eunice's vanity. It's from the thirties with a fancy mirror which has lost its silver in spots. Her collection of potions and lotions sits on a gold tray, waiting for her to return and go through the daily ritual that kept her face and body younger looking than her years. I glimpse my own face in the mirror, my cat face with its inscrutable eyes. What would be there about Eunice, if I could read the human ones behind them? I'm not sure. Something. Anger or pain. A little of both. Maybe even loss. I don't know. I'm out of touch with interpreting human emotion. I put my energies where they serve me now. And emotion? Better off without it.

The smell of roses scents the air. The lid of one of the larger pots, which I know is full of a pale pink potion that would be easy to spread but thick enough to stick, is lying loosely across the top of the jar. It's open. Isn't *that* convenient? Just in case it's a trap Eunice set before she died, I bat at the lid and jump away as it goes end over end onto the floor. But nothing goes poof. That's a good sign.

I creep back up on the pot of face cream, cautious, and it looks okay. It doesn't have to be a trap. Eunice had become forgetful over the last few weeks of her life. At our last supper, she went to the fridge and back three times before she remembered to bring the salad dressing she'd gone there for. It wasn't like her, but I put it down to aging, not to impending doom. As it turns out, her slow decline may have helped me. She would have hated that.

I steel myself against Cat's reaction—he's going to have to deal with a wet paw for a while—and dip my right one into the cream. It's cool, and I'm sure it would feel soothing if Cat weren't going crazy over the wetness of it.

With every bit of concentration I can muster to control the instinct to shake that paw, I make my mark. First, the top part of a capital G. Then, the straight part that hooks up with it and goes down. And then again, after another dip of the paw, the curve at the bottom, and finally, the sticking-in part at the end. I let my paw down and admire my work, leaving an oily spot on the embroidered, antique linen that covers the vanity top.

It's painstaking and difficult, but when it's done, it says "GOOD TOM"—all caps for emphasis—in rose-scented pink lettering with only a few random streaks that don't interfere with the overall message. I think she'll get it this time. Hopefully she'll make it into Eunice's room again soon. I'll need to shadow her closely, stay awake when she's awake. It would be disaster for her to discover my careful work when I'm downstairs napping.

*** 

I weave between the feet of the oldsters who've come to pay their "respects" to Eunice. It seems they're only respectful when Cassie is in earshot. When she isn't, it sounds more like this:

"I don't believe she died a natural death. There are at least ten people in this room alone who would have been justified in killing her..."

"Of course, it's not like she would have cared if we were here or not, but Cassie is a sweet girl..."

"I, for one, am glad the old witch is dead..."

That last one seems to be the consensus. No one but Cassie is going to miss Eunice.

I keep an eye on Natalie, who's been known to discover items from local homes have fallen into her handbag. According to the intel I collected for Eunice, she's had treatment for kleptomania in the past to avoid legal consequences. It wasn't effective. I don't care that she'd steal from Eunice, but the house and everything in it belong to Cassie now. With the exception of Gilly, I'm not sure Cassie should be associating with any of Eunice's old cohorts. Cat has had to gather way too much information about most of them over the years, and frankly, when you look that close at anyone, they're bound to come off at least a little sketchy.

I wend my way to where Cassie is sitting in a chair across from one of the choir members, listening to an old story about Eunice that makes her sound almost human. I scramble onto the expensively upholstered arm, careful not to leave claw marks. Once there, I insinuate myself into Cassie's lap. Her fingers scritch along my spine, then she chucks me under the chin gently to raise my face to hers so that her red-rimmed eyes meet mine.

"Hello, Tom. Are you staying out of trouble?"

Gillian, who's nursing her tea in the chair opposite, asks, almost nonchalantly, although I know her well enough to tell she's bursting with curiosity, "You've renamed him Tom? What inspired that name?"

"I found it written on the inside of his collar. He likes it, so he got a new name." I jump to Gilly's lap and rub my head lovingly against her, then lift my paws to stand with them on her chest, looking up into the green eyes that are looking into mine.

Gilly holds my gaze for a long moment. I can almost see the gears turning. Then, she shakes herself free of whatever thoughts had her frozen and says, "Interesting. Well, Tom is a good name. I was once close with someone named Tom. Although he didn't purr quite so prettily."

Gillian pets me absently as her eyes move up to look behind Cassie. She leans in and says, sotto voce, "Don't look now, but that wanker Kevin is making his way over here."

"Is he? He stopped by earlier this week. He was nice until Tom decided to make a meal of his ankle."

"Well, he would be, love, you're a very attractive girl. Just be wary of him is what I'm saying. Your little Tom seems to have good sense." Gillian leans back and speaks again at normal volume as she turns to the intruder, "Oh, hello, Kevin. Is your father with you?"

"No, no, he's not. He asked me to make his apologies. He had urgent business to see to after the service and will be unable to attend the wake."

Urgent business? More like drowning puppies or evicting the poor from their tenements. Maybe just some gloating and hand-rubbing as he anticipates the nefarious way he'll get his hands on Cassie's property. Having either one of them in the private living area of the house makes me want to spit and hiss, but Gillian soothes my hackles down with a stroke and sets me on the floor, where I sit sentinel. I'm not blinking until he's gone.

Kevin turns to Cassie, "By the way, I know it's still early days, but have you made any firmer plans about whether or not you're staying? I do hope you will."

"Nah, I'm still thinking things over. I always enjoyed working in the shop when I was a kid, but I'm not sure I want to do it as an adult. I just got a degree in Arts Administration, and I'm looking for an opportunity to use it."

"I didn't know that—I'm sure you know our gallery here in town?"

"Absolutely! The Giles Gallery of the Arts was my favorite place when I stayed with Granny Eunice. Mr. Simmons always took time with me to explain about the exhibits and how the art world works. He's the one who inspired me."

"It isn't well-known, but poor Simmons fell on hard times a while back, and my father was good enough to help him through it so that he didn't lose the gallery. Dad and I now own an 80% share. If you're interested in a position there, well— Simmons is getting long in the tooth and would be happy to have help."

"Really? He seemed to still be so full of enthusiasm the last time I visited."

"Oh yes, tired of the working world, as I understand it. Although he wouldn't say that to a potential customer, I'm sure."

Kevin knows much more about those "hard times" than he'd let Cassie in on. He created them for the purpose of him getting his hands on the gallery. Eunice had me do the dirty work in exchange for Kevin making sure his local fuzz buddies look the other way when questionable deliveries come to the shop.

It took me a long time to find something on Simmons. The only thing he's interested in is art, which doesn't normally lead to obvious depravity. Still, you'd be surprised what an enterprising cat can catch a glimpse of in a locked, humidity and temperature controlled room in the basement of an art gallery if he's a stealthy stalker. It turns out Simmons was willing to pay a high price to retrieve a painting that shouldn't have existed, but despite that, magically disappeared from his vault. To get it back, he needed a loan. A hush-hush one which Robert, at Kevin's insistence, was more than happy to make with the lion's share of the gallery as collateral.

When Simmons was eventually unable to repay the loan's steep interest, Robert became the majority partner in the business. I guess Kevin is already anticipating his father's death when he says he owns it.

"If he's really thinking about retiring, I can't think of anything I'd like more than the chance to learn from someone as knowledgeable as Dash

Simmons. I'd be thrilled to do it!"

"Of course, something like that wouldn't leave time to run a shop. Or much time for the upkeep on a big, old Vicky like this one. You'd want to sell it and move to one of the modern homes a little farther from town."

If Cassie moves and takes me with her, I'll be Cat permanently. Nothing can shift me when I'm outside this house. I start to move, but Cassie reaches down to grab me and pulls me into her lap. Maybe she knows I'll be heading for the bastard's leg again. She keeps a firm grip.

Gillian interrupts. She's got a tone of command now that she didn't have when she was young. "Kevin, Cassie's old enough to know her own mind. I'm sure she can sort out her work and living arrangements just fine without any help from you or your father."

"I'm only trying to be supportive, Gillian."

"Of course you are," she replies. Only a trace of sarcasm betrays her.

Natalie and her gang drift closer during the exchange. If they were cats, their ears would have pricked up and swiveled in Kevin's direction to home in on every word coming out of his mouth. From the corner of my eye, I see Natalie's face briefly register disappointment as Kevin heads toward the hall to the kitchenette where the food is laid out. Maybe she wanted to see him get into it with Gillian as much as I did. But Gillian has far too much class to ruin a funeral.

I don't. I'd shut his mouth quick if I could.

As soon as Cassie forgets me and her grip loosens, I slip off her lap and wend my way carefully around the edge of the room, ducking under furniture to avoid the witches tramping around with no concern for the furry familiar at their feet. Kevin is still standing near the food table, in conversation with one of the other witches who was part of the black moon events. Their talk is a low murmur. I don't pick any of it up over the subdued hubbub in the room. Kevin moves off, and I keep him in sight. He's heading for the hall. Could be he needs the bathroom. It could also be he's up to no good.

I track him from a safe distance, waiting a minute before I follow him around the corner, but I find I'm not as stealthy as I think I am. I run right up on his shiny black dress shoes then rise swiftly into the air when he grasps me roughly by the skin at the back of my neck. Cats. Born with handles. Still, it's better than being lifted by the throat.

I dangle half a foot away from his mean, stupid face as he laughs.

"Well, look at that. I've got a tail." He smirks. It reminds me of Eunice. "I'm sure you'll excuse the pun? Now, cat, what do you think I should do with you?"

I hiss, spit, and swish my paws helplessly through the air, my head pulled back at a useless angle from the pressure at the back of my neck. I flail with the white thorns of my claws out, helpless and exposed, and feeling very small. What kind of man feels threatened by a fluffy kitten?

"Kevin? What are you doing?" Cassie hurries to us, although for a moment there, I'd hoped it was Eunice back from the grave so the bastard would get what he deserves. "Give him to me, now!" she demands.

Kevin shoves me toward her, making an excuse, but she won't have it. "You need to leave. This is a funeral. This is my Granny's funeral, and you're hurting a helpless kitten. You're not welcome here today." She pulls me close to cuddle me, tears dropping steadily into my fur, and I watch him go with a feeling of relief.

He shouldn't be here. He should never be here.

CASSIE DUSTS THE SHELVES and rearranges an item here, an item there.

"Well, Tom, I'm leaning toward opening the shop today. I don't think I can go through one more box of old photos, and I can't even think about starting in Granny's room with all her personal things yet."

Even though I want her to find the carefully prepared words I've left for her on Eunice's vanity, I almost hope she's never ready to go through Granny's possessions. A nice girl like Cassie won't even know the names of many of the "personal things" she'll find there. While it's about time Cassie stops thinking of Eunice as a pillar of society, I don't think coming across the adult toys, surveillance equipment, restraints, and other unsavory stuff is the ideal way for it to happen. I'm angry at Eunice for a lot of reasons, but right now,

I'm especially angry at her for dying without wiping away the evidence of her hidden life so that innocent Cassie has to be the one who discovers it.

Cassie opens the till of the old-fashioned cash register and lays out the bills in piles. "There are enough ones and coins here to be able to handle a day's worth of making change. I'm going to take that as a good omen. I guess I should do this thing." She picks me up and plops me in the basket on the counter that has been reserved for "Cat" for over forty years and then walks to the door to turn the lock and flip the sign from "Closed" to "Open."

As she walks back to the counter, she says, "So, are you ready for the onslaught? I'm sure the customers will come crowding in now, right?" Before she finishes her sentence, the door opens behind her, and the shop bell rings. She turns to greet her customer, but I can't see her expression when she identifies him.

"Kevin."

If I were her, I'd add, "And how can we make you turn around and go away?" And then I'd give him a thump on the head for emphasis. Why is he here, lurking around her after she caught him being his awful self in public?

"I'm purchasing, not visiting. My housekeeper swears by Eunice's headache powder, so I like to keep a supply of it available. The poor woman suffers terribly from migraines." When she doesn't respond, he continues, "And I'm also here to give you my heartfelt apology. Your kitten and I don't get along, but an animal can't help acting like an animal. I can. Will you forgive me?"

She shrugs. "Granny made a good headache powder, that's for sure. If your housekeeper needs it, I wouldn't keep her from getting it."

"Thank you. You have to do what you can to help the people who help you. It's just common decency, isn't it?" Kevin smoothes the lonely strands of hair across the top of his head and gives her an oily smile. "Let's see, valerian, and I'll also need a packet of mayapple. For the garden pests, obviously. Natural remedies are best, aren't they?"

"Sure, let's see—headache powder should be over here—yes, I've got it. Valerian and mayapple will be in the herbal remedies section. Do you need the large or the small packets?"

"Large, please. I want to make sure I have enough to get the job done."

If Eunice had taught Cassie more about magic she might have deduced from Kevin's order that the housekeeper's need for headache powder was more than likely caused by Kevin dosing her with a potion of the other two. I remember Eunice having a laugh she didn't bother to hide from him when he bought his first batch of those three powders together. Maybe his order today was a test. If it was, he left the shop knowing just how innocent Cassie is of the goings on in Giles.

While Cassie bags Kevin's purchases, a young

Asian man enters the shop. I recognize him as one of Eunice's less reputable customers. He goes directly to the counter and says in a heavy Chinese accent, "I'm here for Mr. Liu's package." Kevin moves off to the side, his transaction complete, but waits while the man and Cassie talk.

Cassie replies, "I'm sorry. My grandmother, who owned the shop, died last week. I haven't seen a package." Cassie stops for a second, taking a deep breath as tears begin to well up again. "I'll be happy to prepare Mr. Liu's package if you can tell me what he ordered."

The young man looks at her stonily. "No. I need to talk to Mr. Liu before I talk more to you. Mr. Liu may make another arrangement, or he may send me back." He turns and leaves briskly.

Kevin is suddenly in a hurry. He waves a quick goodbye to Cassie and follows the man out of the shop. I scurry after him and coast out the door in his wake. He calls to the man, and they talk briefly, then Kevin hands him his card. It's worse than I thought—Kevin is definitely following through on his plan to move in on the darker side of the business now that Eunice is gone. Too bad for him he doesn't have either the client or supplier list. All that illicit business Eunice keeps locked in the storage room is about to come to an end, and I can't see how Kevin is going to manage to keep it going without some very bad juju going down for Cassie. She has no idea, none at all, how dangerous things could get.

Kevin turns back toward the shop and looks me right in the eye before I scramble back into the recessed doorway. His eyes narrow as he hurries toward me. I mewl like my tail's on fire to get Cassie's attention, and it works. She opens the door and scoops me up, scolding me for ducking out. Back on the counter I go before Kevin can get to me. He peers in the window briefly, then moves on.

*** 

"Granny never let me in to the smaller storeroom, Tom. What do you think I'll find there? Fairy dust? Voodoo dolls?" She smiles weakly at her own attempt at a joke. Her spirits are brighter tonight. It must be a relief to have the funeral out of the way.

What's in the closet, Cassie? A whole lot of trouble, that's what. Without any way to know what Kevin is up to, and, trapped as a cuddly kitten, I've got no way to protect her from what's going to go down if someone comes for the treasure Eunice locked up in there. When an interested party comes to take it, I sincerely hope it's cowardly Kevin instead of a more dangerous threat.

Cassie tries every key on the big metal ring. None of them fit, but I already know that. Eunice used a spell not a lock. The spell won't stop someone who's determined to get in and would remove the door to do it, but it will prevent casual snoopers such as a curious granddaughter or a business rival with a roving eye.

Cassie gives up on the lock and scoops me up on her way upstairs.

***

It's cozy in the upstairs parlor, cuddled up in Cassie's lap while we watch TV. But my thoughts, when I can put a non-Cat thought together, are starting to focus almost entirely around two little words: say it.

I tried the jumping-on-the-table manipulation on Cassie as soon as she knew my real name, but she hasn't had the same response again. Frustrating. I was so sure I'd be freed with a couple of quick jumps. Or failing that, she'd have to go to Eunice's room for something and read the words out loud as I follow her in. But she hasn't ventured into that room. I know. I've been her shadow.

To keep the pressure on, I've been at my most adorable for days, bringing Cassie presents whenever I find something new she might appreciate—mostly things I've batted under furniture over time and Eunice never went searching for. Why in the world can't she just say it? I'm being as good as I know how to be.

All I get as I drop off my packages is:

"Tom, how sweet! I've always wanted a ball of

rubber bands."

"Tom, you shouldn't have! A dusty old spool of thread? Thank you."

"Would you look at that—this must be at least twenty years old. Where did you find it?"

Then, Eureka! I remember something that has to work. I leap from her lap and race into the guest bedroom, then return to the parlor and drop a gold ring on the table in front of her. I just rank a "Where did you get this, Tom? Was it Eunice's?" She slips it idly onto her pinky and twists it as she finishes watching her show.

Why can't she just say it? Just one "good Tom." How hard is that?

I can't tell her that the ring was payment for a potion to precipitate miscarriage. The desperate woman had nothing but her wedding ring to pay with, and the baby she was carrying would have been the wrong color for her husband's genetic background. I thought she would have been better off with the father of the child—the one who cared about her—instead of the one who'd have killed both her and the baby if she'd delivered him a mixed-race child. She lost her ring but got to keep her marriage. I hid it in a fit of pique after watching the glee it gave Eunice. But I can't tell Cassie that. I can't tell her anything.

The longer things go on this way, the fuzzier I feel: I constantly lose focus and get distracted by all the things a cat can find under counters and couches and crawling up the walls. I want to focus on Cassie, but she's becoming less and less interesting unless she's giving me a meal or a scratch.

Cat even gets in on my gift selections because I'm now too instinct driven to stop him. He dropped a dead spider in front of her on the counter this morning. That one earned a "Yuck!" and a quick cleanup.

I crawl back into her lap, discouraged. The words are never going to happen. Never.

"Well, come on Tom, might as well put this ring in Granny's jewelry box for safekeeping." Cassie holds me close as she gets up and turns the TV off.

Eunice's jewelry box is on the vanity. It's finally happening. I feel like I'm floating as we travel along the short upstairs hall together.

And the words are still there, perfectly shaped. I know they are.

Cassie stops dead about three feet from the vanity. "What the?"

I hold my breath. She reads the words.

"6000 ton? This wasn't here before! Who would have snuck in here to write something stupid like that? Are they trying to scare me, make me think Granny's trying to communicate? What does it even mean?"

That's it. I'm done with her. She's a moron.

I get a nice chunk of her arm between my teeth, and she drops me, looking surprised. I show her my backside as I run down the stairs, heading for something satisfying to break or, even better, something to kill.

MOVEMENT UNDER THE BED. I leap to it. It's nothing. Wait...behind me. A crawly. A meal. I bat at it, hold it down, let it up, let it run, bat at it, hold it down, let it up, let it run.

The fun is gone. Crunch it up.

Shine from the window. Warm. Wait...what is it? I turn, I pounce, I turn, I pounce, I turn, I pounce.

"Come on, Tom, stop chasing your own tail. Breakfast time."

I look at her. I know my name. My name is Tom. Good Tom. Say it! Say Good Tom.

I jump along behind her down and down.

Each step down means say it.

Say it. Say it. Say it. Say it. Say it. Say it. Say it.

\*\*\*

I stalk shiny head. He talks. I stalk.

Shoelaces. Pounce. I arch. I spit.

"Tom! What's gotten into you?"

Grabbed. In my cage now.

I'm alert. I keep my eye out. Shiny head talks. Talks and talks.

Cassie helps girl. Shiny head looks. I know you, shiny head. Do you know me?

Cassie comes back. Shiny head talks.

He goes. I'm free again.

I purr, I rub.

Say it. Say it. Good Tom, good Tom, good Tom, good Tom, good Tom, good Tom.

She has the broom. Swickswickswick. She opens the door. One hand on the door. One hand on the broom.

I chase to the door. The smells, oh the smells. I dart to it. Hand grabs. Broom falls. Door closes. Still inside.

"What's wrong with you today? Be good, Tom!"

Oh, it hurts, but it is good tom, good tom, good tom...

I'VE GONE NUTS, right? Granny's kitten starts to stretch and grow and morph. Its little legs start to look like arms at the front and thighs in the back and oh, wow...that's not right to see that on a cat. And in just seconds, my kitten Tom is a naked man with shoulder-length, messy brown hair, green eyes, a smooth chest, thin hips, a smooth, nicely rounded bottom...and well...a naked man! What the hell? I scramble away, backing up fast, afraid to take my eyes off of him.

He twists himself over to sit, his arms wrapped around his knees, rocking, looking up at me and mumbling rhythmically like that homeless, crazy guy in Boston who slept in the alley across from my apartment. It's crazy talk. It sounds like, "say it" and after that it's "goo tah", "goombah", or maybe "gouda"?

How did a bum—a young, buff, naked bum—

get into the shop, and why is he talking about cheese? He gets to his feet, standing there in all his hot hobo glory, and I have no idea what to do, so I just act.

The door's open. I run at him and shove him in the middle of the chest. He staggers back. I push again, and he's outside, and I'm slamming the door closed.

Then the man is changing, shrinking, until it's just poor little Tom out there, looking up at me with pleading green eyes. His meowing is pitiful. But, do I let him in? What's going on?

I know what's going on: I've gone insane. I've lost it. It's the stress, right? My fiancé sleeping with my best friend. The wedding I'd been so busy planning is never going to happen, and the two most important people in my life betrayed me with each other. Then, my favorite Granny dies unexpectedly. Out of nowhere, I own a business and rental cabins and a bunch of other stuff she never even told me about, if Mr. Mayor Robert Andrews, Kreepy Kevin's daddy, told the truth while he talked my ear off today.

It has to be the stress. There's no way I'm talking to a kitten and it suddenly presto-changos into a sexy guy.

I'm having freaky-sexy hallucinations, but whatever my problem is, how can I leave a defenseless kitten out there by himself?

I open the door, but Tom turns and runs after a

scrap of paper as it blows by down the street. I run after him, but he slips through a picket fence and under a porch.

All I can do is stand there calling, "Tom, come here kitty. Kitty, kitty, kitty. Come home!"

I call for a long time, but Tom doesn't come.

I walk back to the shop. The door is standing open for anyone to just walk in and take off with everything in the till. Granny would have given me an earful for that one. I start to tear up for the fifth time today.

*** 

I don't sleep well. I miss Tom's warm body pressing into the small of my back. It's comforting to have him around so that I don't feel so alone. But I am alone, I feel that sharply. My dad always said, to anyone who would listen, that Granny Eunice was a crappy mom which is why he went to his father's to live when he was small, but she was a good grandmother to me, and I loved her. I miss her.

I make breakfast, trying not to feel deranged. Trying not to dwell on the strange things happening in this house: the sexy catman, the weird writing on the vanity mirror, and the scary sounds it makes now that I'm alone in it. Whatever. Too much stress and too much imagination. Why wouldn't I dream up a hot guy and project him out into the real-life world? At least breakfast is completely normal, although I wish Tom was here to eat from his little blue bowl and keep me from feeling so deserted.

If I'm going to make a home here, I want my kitten back. A girl needs another heartbeat in the house.

Did I seriously just say I want to make a home here? You know, I think I did. It's as good a place as any, now that Boston doesn't feel like home any more. I'd spend every day afraid I'd run into Dan or Charlie—or worse—Dan and Charlie.

Even though most of the kids I hung out with during my summer visits have moved away or are at college out of state now, Gilly's an old sweetie, and if Robert really does need someone to run the gallery when Mr. Simmons retires, it would be too good an opportunity to pass up. Well, at least as long as Kreepy Kevin wasn't around all the time. I don't like him one bit. And Gillian told me Daria is back now! She graduated this year and hasn't found a job either. We had fun when we played softball together. I could look her up. We could hang.

After breakfast, I scrabble through the kitchen drawers, looking for any other keys I might have missed. Nothing. I don't want to get a locksmith for the back room, but I can't just leave it locked and not know what's in there if it's related to the shop and its inventory. Omigod, inventory—when do I have to do that for taxes? Is it already done for the year? I haven't even found the accounting books for the business yet.

Okay, that's enough, stop panicking! You'll give yourself another psycho hallucination. Granny wouldn't have left all of this to me if she thought I couldn't handle it. I have to face up to the rest of what needs to get done in the house by going into her room to sort through her things. I refuse to go round-the-bend bonkers again today.

I wash up the breakfast dishes and then head upstairs. I pause in the doorway for a while, taking it in. When I was young, I loved the reds, the crimson satin bedspread that matched the curtains, the lushness of her room. I was a kid. I didn't realize it was decorated in southern gothic whorehouse.

The bed, bedspread, and pillows are gone, the weird writing on the mirror hasn't come back, and the room still smells strongly of disinfectant. Which is lots better than it could smell. Wow, I really didn't need to gross myself out.

How must Gillian have felt walking into the house and knowing right away what was wrong? Not that there was any love lost between her and Granny, but she's been like an extra grandmother to me ever since her husband Marty was my softball coach every summer. She was always there to cheer us on and bring us goodies. They never had kids. I guess they liked borrowing other people's. I know she feels bad for what I'm feeling. She's so kind and so dear.

Once I've cleared the boxes from the top of the closet, and they're sitting neatly in a pile, I pull Granny's plush, bedside chair over and pluck one from the stack. Hats. Granny loved hats. There are three beautiful little pillboxes covered completely in brightly colored feathers. They're exceptional: beautifully preserved, colorful, and amazingly well made. These have to be from the sixties. I appreciate them for a while and then set them aside. Maybe I'll keep one and take the others to a vintage shop. Or maybe I'll just throw them in the attic until I decide what to do with them.

Box number two. Gloves, hankies, brooches, and other pieces of costume jewelry that are tucked up in their original boxes for safekeeping. They're out of style, at least for now, including some extremely ugly things from the eighties, but a few of the rhinestone pieces are just dazzling. I pick out a couple that I want to keep, and the others go back into the box for the vintage shop / attic pile.

I'm getting weepy again. All of Granny's precious things...

Nostalgia isn't going to get me through this. Shake it off, girl.

I pick up the third box.

Whoa! I didn't expect that.

Or that.

Or that.

And, wow, ugh! I'm not even sure I know what that is.

Huh. Granny had a much more interesting history with men than I ever wanted to have to think about. I put the lid back on the box and stuff it into a waiting trash bag. If there's something of value in there, it can stay a secret.

With that, I need a cup of coffee.

I check the upstairs kitchen, but it's just tea up here. I have better luck in the downstairs kitchenette, so I get a pot brewing.

I hear a slight sound, a high-pitched cry. I poke my head into the hallway and look out to the shop—there's Tom, with his little paws pressed up against the door glass, looking back at me expectantly. Well, thank goodness.

"So, where have you been all night?" I ask as I open the door. Tom sits there proudly with a dead mouse at his feet. "Yeah...not really my kind of gift, Tom. I preferred the jewelry."

I pick the mouse up by its tail and flick it out into the street, where it lands with a soft, meaty smack. Tom blinks at that, but he gets up and walks into the shop. He follows me into the kitchenette, where I fill his bowl with something I hope is better than the mouse I rejected. He soon has his nose deep in his food and is fully engaged in his meal like nothing freaky ever happened.

Because nothing did happen. It couldn't have. Whatever insanity grabbed me yesterday is far away now. I've had a good night's sleep and what was obviously transient psychosis precipitated by my exhaustion and stress has passed. I give Tom's little ears a scratch, and he has a hard time trying to decide if he should eat or purr. The solution he comes up with sounds like a broken engine as he purrs, then swallows, then revs up again.

\*\*\*

I'm sorting through another box from Granny's closet when Tom joins me from downstairs. He's playful this morning, that's for sure. He decides to do some sorting of his own, pushing the lid off a shoebox and managing to tip it over so that the photographs inside come spilling out. Oh well, he's not hurting anything spilling boxes of photos. They'll be easy enough to pick up later.

I'm sorting through the clothes in Granny's closet, separating the beautifully preserved vintage stuff—there's a lot of that—from the modern day-to-day stuff that can go to Goodwill. There are also some men's clothes pushed to the side of the closet: an embroidered red satin robe, a couple of pairs of bell-bottom jeans, a turtle-neck, and two colorful, loose cotton shirts. Dashikis? I think that's what they called them.

Looks like her boyfriend was kind of a hippie. I wouldn't have guessed that. Granny Eunice was such a Daughters of the American Revolution type. Very classic, very buttoned down. There are a lot of surprises tucked away in here.

I nearly step on Tom when I turn away from the closet with an armful of clothes. He's looking up at me with a photograph in his mouth. Another present? Better than the mouse, I hope.

I reach down to take it, and he drops it on the floor at my feet. When I pick it up, I see it's a picture of Granny in the sixties. She's with two other people, leaning against the fender of a classic car. Granny is wearing a tailored skirt and sweater set. And wait—the other woman is Gillian. Omigod, she's such a hippie! And next to her is a handsome guy with longish, curly brown hair, wearing a brightly patterned dashiki.

No. Freaking. Way.

I'm holding that dashiki draped over my arm, and although it can't be possible, the guy in the picture is the guy I pushed out the shop door last night.

I put the clothes on top of the cedar chest and turn back to the closet. My imagination can do what it wants. I'm going to ignore it. I'm just going to keep sorting things and pay no attention to the ghosts. Tom meows furiously, but I shut it out.

IT'S GOOD TO BE dealing with the day to day problems of the shop instead of having my imagination run wild and take me with it. Stock of a few herbals is running low, so I put in a call to Granny's supplier. With it just turning spring here, I can't source a lot of the herbs locally, but once summer is in full swing, I'll be able to get a lot of the raw ingredients and single herbs that are stocked in the shop from local gardens. I realize I do know an awful lot about the business as I get to work. I had no idea I was paying that much attention during those summers I spent here.

I decide to give Gillian a quick call so I can ask her about the guy in the picture before I open up. Not that I believe I saw him the other night any more than I believe Granny's writing me cryptic messages about 6000 tons of something from beyond the grave, or even that somebody in town wrote it to freak me out. It was probably there before, and I didn't notice. It's just stress. None of it is supernatural.

And the picture? It's just a piece of Granny's history I want to fill in. I mean, she's got this guy's clothes in her closet, so what happened to him? And why did she keep his stuff so long? Did he die, and she couldn't give them up? I can't see Granny being that sentimental. I mean, I loved her, but she wasn't anyone you'd call a warm person.

Gillian doesn't pick up, so I leave a message to give me a call whenever.

The shop is busy today with a slow but steady stream of tourists wandering in and then wandering back out. With the better weather, Giles is starting to get a decent number of weekend visitors through town for the gallery and antique shops. That's another thing I have to do! I need to find a caretaker for the cabins and get them ready to open for the summer—Granny's records indicate they're fully booked through the fall already. I don't even know who Granny's had as a caretaker for the past few years since Joshua retired.

Whatever. Another thing on the list that I need to get on paper before I forget it. Sure. The minute I've got these candles bagged and six ounces of fresh fennel measured out and packaged up nice times ten. The second I get a break, I'm on it. It's good that I'm busy. At least I'm no longer crying nonstop.

Kevin and Robert walk in the door just as I've got that second to myself and am picking up a pen for my to-do list.

"Hi Robert," I say, "What's the haps?" Honestly, I wish they'd just turn around and go back out. Robert's fine. I like him when he's on his own, but Kreepy Kevin is well, creepy. He's around my dad's age but he stands way too close to me, and I can feel his eyes burning into my ass every time I turn away from him. Still, the Andrewses own most of the town. If I'm going to be staying, I have to be nice.

Kevin replies, "We're great, Cass. I just wanted to bring Dad by because he's had a talk with Mr. Simmons, and it looks like you could go right into training to take over the gallery. He expects to retire within the year. What do you think?"

"Ummm...wow. It would be a great opportunity, but..."

Robert cocks his head, "You're not interested? Kevin led me to believe…"

"Truthfully, while we talked about it, I haven't had a second to think. I'm still going through the house, and with the shop open again and getting the cabins ready because they're completely booked for the summer..."

Kevin's scary grin droops at the corners. I don't think he's happy with me. What did he think? I'd make snap decisions and just give up all of Granny's history because he offers me a job? He's leering now, and I step back from the yuckness he's broadcasting when he says, "I was under the impression you were excited about it—after I sold Dad on the idea, it's disappointing for you to suddenly change your mind."

Not like I actually did that. Wow. But he's looking at me with squinched-up eyes, and I'm not feeling my most relaxed right now, that's for sure.

Robert steps in then, "We'd be happy to give you a fair offer on the shop and campgrounds to take them off your hands immediately, if that's what you're worried about."

"I...yeah, I need more time. I haven't even gotten Granny's personal things sorted out, much less dug into what the businesses are worth. I'm sure you understand?"

Kevin's grin is entirely forced now. But he tries to keep up the front. "Sure, sure. We can give her a little more time, can't we, Dad? Simmons will still have time to get her trained, particularly since he isn't retiring until the end of the year. But you don't want to let it go too long. We have other options."

Why does that sound like a threat?

Robert smiles, not threatening at all. These guys are like night and day. "I don't see a problem with waiting. I admit I got excited when Kevin told me someone with a relationship to the town has the qualifications to take on the gallery. It's always nice when we can keep these things 'in the family', so to speak. But I see enthusiasm has caused him to get carried away and put the cart before the horse. Of course, take as much time as you need."

"Thanks guys," I say, really only talking to Robert, because Kevin is still trying to pretend he's being nice instead of glaring and leering and generally giving me a case of shivering icks. "It's not that I don't appreciate the offer."

I see Tom stalking toward Kevin out of the corner of my eye. I don't want to risk him getting hurt, so I walk over and grab him just as he's getting ready to pounce. He bats at me with his little claws out.

"I see you're learning that kitten is much wilder than most of Eunice's cats have been," Kevin says, giving his opinion without being asked, as I give Tom a stern look for the scratch he's left on the back of my hand.

"Yeah, I don't know what's gotten into him."

"If he's going to continue attacking your customers, you can't afford to leave him in the shop. Bad for business. Plus, well...left alone with Eunice like that, are you sure he didn't get...how do I say this delicately? Hungry?"

I'm completely grossed out now. I don't like what Kevin just made me imagine about Tom, about Granny. My stomach churns, and I set Tom on the counter as I run for the bathroom in the back. I throw up for what seems like an extra long time.

I rinse my mouth out several times when I'm done and wash my face to get rid of the watery-eyes-because-I've-just-been-sick look and return to the front of the shop, hoping that the Andrewses have taken off. But no, Robert's still standing where I left him, although Kevin is behind the counter, appearing to have come from the direction of the storerooms. What business does he have back there? Absolutely none, as far as I'm concerned.

In response to my curious look, Kevin says, "I apologize for taking the liberty, but I went to the storeroom to look for the monthly package Eunice puts aside for a friend of mine. It's rather a large package, and very heavy, so I'd usually pick it up so she didn't have to. I can't get into the far storeroom, though. I assume you have the key?"

I don't believe him, but it doesn't matter. "No, I don't have a key. That's another of the things I have to sort out. I'm going to get a locksmith next week. What's your friend's name? I'll call you if I find a package."

"Oh, it's..." he pauses in a way I find suspicious, like he doesn't actually have a name to give me, "Keisha, my housekeeper." Boy, he and that housekeeper sure must be close if he's running errands for her all the time. He continues, "And yes, I'd appreciate it if you'd give me a call. Well, Dad, we've probably upset the apple cart enough today."

"I agree. And Cassie, I apologize for my son. I don't know what could have possessed him to say what he did about your kitten." Kevin glares at his father now instead of me, so that's a nice change.

"Please accept my apology, and don't let it prevent you from considering the offer about the gallery. I'd be disappointed if his thoughtlessness prevented you from accepting a position so well suited to your interests."

" I'll think about it, Robert."

We make our goodbyes, but I'm liking those guys less and less. Talk about pushy. And what the heck was Kevin really doing in the back?

Suddenly, I have to squeeze my eyes shut to get rid of the horrific image of what he suggested Tom might have done to Granny. Did he? How can I keep him if he did? I'll never be able to stop thinking about it. I really need to talk to Gillian.

When I turn to where Tom is still sitting on the counter, his little head shakes back and forth and back and forth like he's denying the charges. Like he knows what we were talking about. I know what Kevin said shouldn't influence how I feel about him, but I scoop him up and put him in his cage just the same.

***

Gillian's face is tight and angry. "I can't believe those two! What a couple of wankers! No, Tom did not turn on Eunice after she died. He took a bite out of me when I found him, though. That's how hungry he was. And the medical examiner said there was no sign of any marks on her skin before or after death. The poor little thing did absolutely nothing improper. You have no idea how unusual that is for a cat. They're just not loyal to dead owners the way dogs are."

I set a cup of tea in front of her and sit down across from her at the small table in the kitchenette. "That's good to know. I...well, I couldn't keep him..."

"I understand. That's why I specifically asked about it before the medical examiner left. I'd have had no problem seeing that he disappeared to a nice farm with no one the wiser. I can't imagine why Kevin would even suggest it unless he was just manipulating you to try to get you to move on."

"Robert said he'd be glad to make an offer on Eunice's businesses."

Gillian rolls her eyes. "Yes, of course, he would. He's been trying to buy Eunice out for years. She was the only obstacle in the way of him owning everything worth having in Giles. I won't blame you if you sell, but I wouldn't want to see it happen."

"Why not?"

"Cassie, there are forces at work in Giles you don't know anything about. As they say, ignorance is bliss."

"Yeah, well, I'm not exactly blissful right now. And if I'm really going to stay, you should clue me in."

Gillian looks at her hands. Her jaw works back and forth while she thinks. Then she obviously makes a decision because she says, "I'll spill it if I must...because if you sell to the Andrewses, it will upset a delicate balance in Giles. As long as Robert is alive, I have hope things won't go down a bad path. But once Kevin inherits..."

I wait, but she's holding back again. Now I'm extra curious about this dark secret in boring little Giles. "Gillian!"

She sighs a huge sigh. "Yes, all right. Whether or not you stay, you should understand about your grandmother, me, Giles, and your legacy. It's not just city politics."

"So...what is it? What's the big mystery?"

She looks me directly in the eye.

"Cassie, I'm a witch, your grandmother was a witch, Robert and Kevin are warlocks, and although you don't know it yet, I'm betting you're a witch, too. Robert is our high priest, and Eunice was our high priestess. They've had equal power and kept each other in check all these years. But now, that balance is threatened. Natalie will become our high priestess on the next new moon, but she can only restore balance within the coven. She can't keep the balance in the town."

Huh. Okay, so basically, not only have I gone insane and started seeing things, but my only friend in town is just as short of a full deck as I am. She waits for my reaction quietly, her face wearing her usual, kind expression. Nothing to hint that she's an escaped lunatic or gone utterly senile.

I figure I have to say something. I can't just continue staring at her. I take the picture of Granny, Gillian, and the handsome stranger out of my pocket and push it across the table to her. "Give me time to think about that. It's a lot to take in. I actually called you because I wanted to ask you who's in this picture with you and Gran."

Gillian takes the photo, and her lip quivers a little as her smile fades. "That's my ex-husband, Tom. He disappeared after having an affair with your grandmother. She drove him away. Or, lately, since Eunice's death, I've had the feeling that maybe he never left at all."

Huh.

I sit there and wait for her to say more, my heart racing, but my face blank. Nothing to hint that I'm an escaped lunatic or gone utterly senile.

Gilly stays where she drifted off to, her expression telling me her thoughts are far away.

I'm afraid of the question, but I ask it anyway. "Gilly, where do you think your ex-husband is?"

She looks back at me, and, dead serious, says, "There's no way to ease into this, sweetheart, so I'm just going to say it. Where's your cat?"

***

Gillian and I stand behind the counter, looking at Tom in his cage.

"So, the part about everybody being witches,

that's true?"

"I'm afraid it is."

"And the reason you think I'm a witch?"

"Because you made a good portion of the potions in this shop, and they work just fine. Better than fine. Eunice raised you in real magic but told you it was herbal medicine or tourist magic. It wasn't."

It's exhaustion psychosis again; I know it. But what the heck, I'll go along with it. "I see. And the reason you think my Tom is your Tom?"

"The collar. Tom's name in Eunice's handwriting. It would be just like Eunice to do something like this if she had the power to do it, and I believe she had more power than any of us knew. She had a lot of secrets."

I nod to myself, thinking. Wait, what? I'm acting like this could really happen. Yeah, I guess I am. Might as well go for the whole enchilada. "Hang out for another minute, Gilly," I say.

I hurry up the stairs and gather the men's clothes I found in the closet. When I return, I set them on the counter.

"Are these Tom's?"

She looks sad again. "Yes. His favorite trousers and shirts. They went missing from the house the same day I found the note telling me he was leaving me. I don't recognize the robe, though."

There's silence for a while, then I finally break it. "I'm sorry, Gilly."

"Don't be. Tom and I were young. A few years after he disappeared, I divorced him and got on with life. I had my Martin, as you know, until he passed four years ago. I never forgot Tom—you don't forget your first—but in Martin, I met someone wonderful who gave me all the love I could possibly handle. I just couldn't help brawling with Eunice about it once in a while."

"Marty was a great guy." I put a hand on her shoulder. "And Tom? That's what those fights were about? The ones that always stopped so suddenly when I walked into the room?"

"Yes, dear. Not a fit topic for a young girl to overhear."

"Gilly, I have to tell you this...a few nights ago—well, really, I thought I'd just lost my mind from the stress—Tom was a dead kitten one minute and a live, naked man the next. I freaked. I shoved him out the door, and then he was kitten Tom again. He's the one who brought me that picture. And that was him, the man I saw was the man in the picture. I guess I should let him out of the cage?"

"Yes. Yes, I think you should. Although I haven't an inkling how we'd go about finding out if it's true."

I open the cage and Tom hurries out, wending his way between us, rubbing against our legs.

Gillian leans down and says, "So, what do you think we should do with you?"

Tom doesn't answer as he rubs his face against her outstretched hand over and over and over.

WHEN TOM SETTLES into the small of my back for the night, I move him onto the bedside chair. He looks a little put out before he curls up with his tail tucked in.

"Sorry, Tom. But I don't feel comfortable snuggling up with you. Because, wow, you're freaking hot for a kitten." I laugh at myself now, because I'm totally bonkers.

I swear he nods just like all the crazy talk about him being a man is true. Then he curls up for the night. I curl up, too, trying to ignore that I just moved a cat off the bed because I'm afraid he'll turn into a pinup boy from my steamiest fantasies. The temporary psychosis I apparently share with Gillian is obviously working on becoming permanent.

I wake up to a sound downstairs, just a slight shuffling, but the recent spooky stuff has me waking at every noise. I look to the chair, but Tom is gone.

It must be him I hear, prowling around below. I lay back down, but now I'm alert and vigilant, and every creak as the house adjusts to the wind and temperature sounds suspicious. Alright, I'm getting up. I'm not going to be able to sleep until I satisfy myself there's nothing there.

I go to the closet and get my old summer-league softball bat and move down the stairs, trying not to hyperventilate. I'm going for stealth. Definitely not a good time to pass out from anxiety. As I enter the shop and look around, I see movement in the short hall that leads to the storerooms. And then I hear Tom hissing, followed by a sudden, piercing yowl.

Someone's back there, and he's hurting Tom; I'm sure of it. My hand tightens on the bat as my legs tense and I move forward.

I run past the counter, bat raised, screaming, "Get the hell out of my shop!"

There's no one there, no one that I can see as I scan the dark room. But I know I'm not alone. It stinks of nervous sweat in here. I rushed to Tom's defense, but where is he? I don't see him anywhere. Then there's a squeal, and I see Tom in the gloom by the far storeroom door, lying on his side, not moving.

I move toward him and someone pushes me back, but I still don't see anyone. It's dark but not that dark. Where is he? I bring the bat crashing down where a body would be if there was one attached to whoever pushed me. A man yelps in pain before he knocks me down, and the sound of footsteps on the creaky floor race toward the door. It opens and then slams closed.

I half-slide/half-crawl to the storeroom door. Tom is on his side in front of it, breathing shallowly, blood matting the fur of his tiny face and chest, his face contorted. Oh no, oh terrible. Poor Tom.

As I try to look him over without causing greater damage, he stops breathing altogether. His little body relaxes, and I know he's gone.

My chest tightens as the sobs start. My grandmother, Dan, my best friend, all gone. My father can't even show me support by coming to Granny's funeral, and finally, my kitten gets taken away.

And now there are whimpers, but they're not mine. I open my eyes, and Tom's body is changing, morphing, growing, like before. It's wrong and gross and weird, but it's mesmerizing to watch as man parts sprout out-of-proportion to cat parts, then the rest of his body catches up as what was condensed becomes uncondensed. I step back, and when the change is complete, the man from the photos—Gillian's husband—huddles there in all his masculine glory.

He looks right at me and says slowly, pleadingly, and carefully, "Say good Tom. Say good Tom. Just say it."

Then his body contracts again suddenly,

collapsing back in on itself, growing fur, turning into a fluffy black ball, and there's a young kitten there again. What the?

So, the hot bum wasn't a cheese fan. And nobody wrote "6000 ton" on the vanity. And this is the third time he's told me what to say.

Alright, I'll just say it. But what am I expecting will happen?

"Good Tom."

*** 

The clothes I'd brought down for Gillian to see are still sitting on the table in the kitchenette. I dash in there and come out with the whole stack, placing them on the ground and pushing them toward the man, Tom—I guess I'll have to get comfortable with calling him   that. Or get hauled to the nuthouse, one of the two. He's curled up into a ball just like a cat, his eyes closed. In pain? Disoriented?

"I brought you some clothes."

He opens his eyes and grabs for the robe, treating his hands like paws. He sits up and fiddles with it but can't figure out the sleeves. He looks frustrated and lowers his head, shaking it, and then lifting it and trying again. "Cat long time. A long time. Help."

I really don't want to get near him.

"Please help."

He looks so vulnerable. I grab the robe and take

one of his hands, "Stand up. It'll be easier."

He stands up jerkily, balancing until the last minute with his other hand in addition to his legs.

I help him feed one arm into a sleeve and then tell him to turn so that I can reach his other hand and feed that one into a sleeve as well. From there, he manages to pull the robe on, closing it in the front and even managing to tie the belt to hold it that way.

"Kevin. It was Kevin," he says.

"I have to make a call," I say.

\*\*\*

Gillian walks into the sitting room, and her eyes fill with tears when she sees Tom curled up on the couch in his bright-red robe.

"Hello, Tom," she squeaks out as she loses control of her voice, and the tears spill out over her cheeks. Then she shrugs it off, her expression hardening as her tears dry. It's like a wall just went up on the other side of her eyes.

Tom looks up at her, his own eyes misting. "Gilly. Sorry. So sorry."

She sits next to him on the couch, and he raises himself on one arm, rubbing his head against her shoulder. "Sorry, sorry, sorry," he croons, more a purr than an apology.

"I'm sorry, Gilly, but it seems like he's more cat than man right now. Or, at least, I'm assuming he wasn't like this before?"

Gilly bursts out laughing. It goes on for a long time. I figure we'll be discovered and taken away to have our brains adjusted any minute, so she might as well laugh while she can.

As she works to get herself under control, she gasps, pulling a long breath, and says, "No, no, he wasn't more cat than man when I married him. Thanks for asking, though."

"Yeah, sorry. I guess that was a stupid thing to say."

"Sweetheart, it's not like this is a situation anyone could be prepared for. We'll just need to make it up as we go along."

She turns to Tom, all business now. "Tom, have you been here all along? Ever since you wrote me that letter?"

Tom nods. "Yes."

"Did Eunice do this to you?"

He nods again. "Yes."

"Tom, you're different now than you were when I knew you."

"Cat too long."

"Will you get better?"

Tom nods his head up and down. Then he says, "Don't say it. Bad Tom."

I look to Gillian. "I changed him back into a man by saying 'good Tom'. It must be the opposite that turns him into a cat. But I didn't say it when I pushed him out of the house that night."

Tom responds. "Trapped in house. Spell."

"Oh, I..." I stop and gather my thoughts. "Gilly, can I talk to you in private?"

She follows me into the kitchenette, and I pull the pocket door closed so Tom can't overhear. "I kind of hoped that you'd take him to your house. But not if he's trapped here. I...this is way too weird for me. I don't want him here. It's freaking me out."

"Well, buck up, sweetheart. He isn't my responsibility any more. I divorced him over forty years ago, and he ended up this way because he cheated on me and broke my heart." She stops and takes a deep breath before she continues. I think she's struggling to put that wall back in place. "No, like the shop and her other properties, he's part of Eunice's legacy now."

"Gillian, I can't..."

"Don't be a child," she snaps. "Of course you can. And what if Kevin comes back? You need a backup, I'd say. One little girl with a bat isn't scary for long."

"Okay. I get it. No decisions tonight. But why should I even believe that it was Kevin? Because my cat said so? I didn't see anyone. So just think on it. Please?" I ask. Still, I'm pissed at her and it surprises me. I think this is the first time I've ever been mad at Gillian. I've never known her to be so mean.

"I'm not going to change my mind. I'll help you try to free him from what your grandmother did so he can go on his way, but I won't take him off your hands."

Well, thanks, Granny Eunice. And thanks, used-to-be-sweet Gillian. Because I'm ready for all of this. Sure I am.

I MAKE UP THE BED in the guest bedroom for Tom, and he snuggles in, looking contented. Gillian left, but she gave a promise to return in the morning. I think she'd calmed down. When she said goodbye to Tom, her expression was wistful instead of angry.

So, time to put on my big girl pants. I've been living with this guy, Tom, in the house since I got here. Since the first time I ever visited Gran. I just need to wrap my head around it in a different way than before.

I hear him moving around in the rooms below me when I wake up. I walk downstairs and see he's managed to dress himself in a pair of his jeans and a shirt, so he's functioning better than yesterday when he couldn't even manage the robe on his own.

I'm not sure what to say, so I go for the obvious. "Morning, Tom."

He startles, then says, "Morning, Cassie." His

speech is better, more normal sounding, less meow-like. So, that's good.

"You want breakfast?"

"Yes, thank you." At least he's polite.

I sort out bacon and eggs and pour him a glass of orange juice. He starts to lap at it with his tongue, then looks like he's concentrating hard, picks up the glass, and drinks it down quickly. I wonder if he's going to push his face into the food, but, with another burst of stiff concentration, he picks up his fork and carefully lifts the food from the plate to his mouth, getting faster and looser the more practice he gets.

"Sorry I scared you. Cat too long. I become Cat. Have trouble thinking."

I figure I might as well start the interrogation even though Gilly isn't here yet. What else are we going to talk about?

"Are you sure it was Kevin last night?" I ask. "Did you see his face? Because I never got a look at him before he knocked me over. I just smelled that nervous sweat, and maybe valerian?"

"Yes, Kevin. But all covered. Only smelled him."

"Kreepy Kevin. But why?"

"Storeroom. Secret packages. Illegal trade. Potent magic. Gilly can get you in. Good with locks. Magic locks." Tom rubs his eyes with the back of his hand and looks tired after his long string of words.

"Is that why there's no key?"

"Yes. Magic to lock it. Magic to open it. Not

safe. Get rid of stuff. All stuff."

"Great...yeah, I'll put it on the to-do list."

"I want you to be safe." Tom's green eyes look so sincere. My loyal kitten, right? Protecting me again. He reaches for my hand where it rests on the table and squeezes it gently. "I want you to be safe."

Well, that doesn't feel at all kitteny. I pull my hand away.

"Let's finish eating, and then Gillian will be here, and we can see how good she is with that lock."

"Tape!" Tom bursts out then. "Tape!" He walks behind the counter and shoves aside the box that covers granny's digital recording system. The lights are green because we've been moving around and it's on a motion sensor.

I run the recording back, and there it is: a man comes in through the shop door, completely covered in a set of black coveralls. He heads for the storeroom. Tom attacks. The intruder kicks him viciously over and over again, then turns when I come in. How is it possible I didn't see him? I mean, I know the tape is on infrared, but there was enough light for me to see Tom. Why couldn't I see the man who was standing right in front of me?

***

Just a few blue sparks from Gillian's fingertips and the storeroom door is open. We walk inside and take inventory of the shelves silently. She turns to me with unease settling into her face.

"Cassie, this is very bad magic. Tom's right about getting it out of here before someone comes for it. I'm also still not happy about invisible prowlers whether or not we think we know who he was."

I pick up the jars and read the labels—tiger penis, rhino horn, giraffe brain—all the stuff you hear about that poachers are killing endangered species for. "Wow. I agree, but how do we do that?"

"Box it up, dear. I've got the SUV. We can take it out to the ritual grounds and destroy it."

Tom has been quiet, waiting outside the storeroom door, but he rouses then. "Won't stop Kevin coming back."

"No, it won't. You're right, Tom. I guess we'll call him and tell him where to find us while we burn it." Tom starts to object, but Gillian shushes him. "Tom, I can take care of myself, and Cassie, too, against someone like Kevin. We'll be fine. Are the client and supplier lists somewhere?"

I pick up a stack of paper and rifle through it. "Yeah, it looks like this is it. At least, these aren't suppliers or customers I ever met or ordered from when I worked here. That guy who sent someone for a package the other day, Mr. Liu? He's on here."

"Good," Gillian says. "We throw that in the fire once we've got Kevin's attention. He needs to know that there's nothing to save from Eunice's little business on the side. Then maybe there won't be any more problems in the shop at night.

"Yeah, but that won't stop the clients coming in, will it?" I ask. Going on to answer myself, I say, "It won't. So before we destroy that list, I'm going to call everyone on there and tell them they'll need to find another place to shop."

Gillian gives me a smile. "Now you're thinking like Marty's star shortstop! I knew you could handle it."

Maybe. But no matter what, we've got a long day ahead of us.

Tom helps Gillian pack up the contents of the storeroom in boxes while I make the calls. I mostly get answering machines, so that makes my job easier. I say my grandmother has died, the business has changed hands, there will be no more packages, and the stock has been destroyed. I work my way through the list of thirty or so customers pretty quickly.

I can hear Tom and Gillian talking softly while they work. I wonder what they say to each other after all these years. I can't even begin to guess, but it sounds private, intimate. Even though they were married, he looks young enough to be her grandson, if she had a grandson with broad shoulders, slim hips, and a perfectly rounded butt. Not to mention sexy green eyes with a hint of mystery hanging out over a smirky smile.

What I mean is that there's not much chance of them getting back together now, even if she does forgive him. That's the only reason I even notice what he looks like.

\*\*\*

I'd been out to the big clearing in Corey woods lots of times, but I never knew it was the ritual grounds for the coven. Gillian fills me in on this part of my heritage as we drive out to the south side of town at dusk in her old Land Rover, the boxes of dangerous stock piled up in back.

Gillian starts a fire in the central pit while I carry the boxes from the truck to sit beside it. She gets a good start, and after I've got the boxes ready, I go off into the woods to grab some bigger pieces of dry wood to really stoke it up.

With the extra wood, the bonfire is huge. "So, what do you think?"

Gilly empties a jar into the flames, and the contents sizzle. "I think it's time you called Kevin."

I take a deep breath and steel myself for it. I'm not much of one for bravery, but it's all wrapped up together, isn't it? The things Granny Eunice did. The things that Kevin and Robert knew about and want to take over. It's hard for me to think of Granny being someone who would make Tom a slave or trade in endangered species, but the evidence is all around me.

I always jumped when Granny said jump. She had such confidence—I admired her so much.

Maybe it's time for me to grow up and talk back to what is clearly a wrong picture of who she was. I pull up the contact I made for Kevin from Granny's rolodex before we left the house and bring the phone to my mouth.

"Kevin? You need to come out to the ritual grounds. We're burning a few things you tried to get your hands on the other night. Thought you might like to say goodbye to them."

"What? What?" he splutters in that icky-oily voice of his.

"Hanging up now. You really need to get here before everything goes up in smoke."

I disconnect and start filming as Gillian empties the contents of jars, plastic bags, and boxes into the flames, naming their contents as she does. The video is a backup in case Kevin doesn't show up in time.

Did I worry that Kevin wouldn't show up? Really? What was I thinking? His classic silver Merc comes barreling down the road. He nearly plows it into Gillian's parked SUV when he slams on the breaks and the car slides on the loose gravel. Kevin hops out the driver side and starts briskly toward us as Robert exits from the passenger side more slowly.

"What the hell are you doing? Do you know what that stock is worth?" In the reflected firelight, his comb-over catches a breeze, and the long strands stand straight up above a face contorted with rage. So there's the Kevin who was lurking behind that constant smile. Definitely a whole different guy than he pretends to be.

"I do. But it's my inheritance, isn't it? And I don't want an inheritance like this." I turn toward my partner in crime and indicate the jar she's holding. "What's that one, Gilly?"

"Giraffe something. Brains? She opens the jar and tosses the contents into the fire. "It might as well be sweetbreads, now, though. And I do think that's the last of it."

I pull the folded sheets of supplier and customer names out of my back pocket, keeping an eye on Kevin as he stalks closer with Robert behind him. He yelps and grabs his left shoulder, his face contorting in pain, when he runs smack into the barrier Gillian put up before they got here. His over-the-top reaction is proof positive it was him I nailed with my turn at bat. It was difficult for me to believe something I couldn't see would keep him out just as it was difficult to believe that someone I couldn't see could be in the shop, but I'm no longer worried. Gillian has got to teach me that. I smile as Robert pulls up short behind him.

"I see you've run into a barrier, there, boys. Too bad. I guess you won't be able to stop us burning the customer list, then." I turn and hand the sheaf of papers to Gillian, smiling. "Gillian, would you do the honors?"

We share a smile as she takes half the papers, and we feed them into the fire sheet by sheet, giving each one a flourish on the way to the flame. It doesn't take long, but boy, are we having fun.

I turn back to where Kreepy stands, still spluttering. "Okay. That was the last of it. The client and supplier names. There's nothing you might want in my little shop now, so don't break in any more, okay? If you decide to try it, I've still got my bat, and I bet I could score a good hit on your other shoulder, too. Plus, I don't think I'll be giving up Corey Woods, either. It seems I have a heritage here that I never knew about. And I've decided I'm going to stick around and become more familiar with it."

Robert is talking under his breath to Kevin now, and from what I catch, it isn't pretty.

Kevin starts to say something, but his father cuts him off. "I'll handle this." Then he turns to face me. "You're right. There's no longer anything in the shop Kevin might want. I want you to know that I didn't know what he'd done until just now. My apologies for any damage he caused in the store. We'll be on our way." He turns to Kevin, "Come on. We're done here," and stalks to the car, refusing to look at his son further.

"Oh my," says Gillian as the Merc throws up a scatter of pebbles when it backs around to leave, "I think we may have touched off a family squabble."

"Yeah, looks like. I know I feel real sorry about that." Gillian and I grin at each other like the madwomen we are.

She puts her arm around me and flings her other hand out toward the barrier. There's a slight sizzling sound as it dissolves.

Oh yeah, she is so going to teach me that. I don't care how crazy this is, because it's crazy exciting, too.

I'm in.

"THAT'S TAKEN CARE OF," says Tom, as he finishes mashing the fennel in the mortar and dumps it into a jar, putting the scoop back on top before he seals it back up with the lid. "All the loose herb jars are filled, and I rearranged the storerooms now that there's some extra space. I put the perishables in the small storeroom to take advantage of the dehumidification and separate thermostat."

"Thanks. Good idea," I say, as Tom turns and heads down the hall. He doesn't seem to have any problem expressing himself now that's he's been human for a few days, and he's been super helpful with a lot of stuff around the house and shop. He's even teaching me what all the herbs and potions can be used for when they're infused with magic. He doesn't have any magic of his own, not since Eunice did to him what she did, but Gillian says she'll teach me how to use mine, so I've been taking notes.

I watch him walk toward the parlor where he'll stay out of sight while the shop is open. I can't help but admire the way his jeans fit. More men should wear bell bottoms. It's a look.

Omigod. Where's my brain? I just snuck a look at the butt of a guy who's in his sixties or something—Gillian's age, at least. And he's Gillian's ex-husband. I should have my eyes removed and burned, shouldn't I? But, well, I've seen Tom in the raw a couple of times now, and Gilly was one lucky woman. And it's not like Tom looks or acts like he's sixty.

I think about Dan now, force of habit, I guess, and how he would look just as yummy in bell bottoms with his short, blonde hair, killer tan, and sculpted abs. Suddenly, I miss him intensely. I miss the way he held me and the way his eyes crinkled at the corners when he smiled. I miss his arm thrown across my body as I sleep. I miss everything about him in a big, giant ache. I press my eyes shut for a minute. I force myself to remember how badly he hurt me. Otherwise, I'd take out my phone and hit the call button.

\*\*\*

I'm thinking about what to make for dinner while I look up when Tom calls from the back, "Hey, I've got a surprise for you. Come upstairs when you're done."

Can't imagine what it might be. At least he's not dropping mice at my feet any more.

I walk up the stairs, and I see he's moved the kitchen table into the living room. It's laid out with Granny's best dining things—fancy linen table cloth, silver candlesticks with candles lit, and the good tableware, including a classy sixties white bone china with a simple platinum rim. The goblets are similarly rimmed with platinum. It looks gorgeous. There's a lovely smell coming out of the kitchen, too, but I have to tease him.

"Wow, Tom, you put a lot of work into this! And you cooked, right? Because it wouldn't be much of a surprise if I have to spend hours in the kitchen making something good enough to put on this table."

He stands in the kitchen doorway, one of Granny's old frilly aprons tied on over his sixties garb with that lopsided, sexy smirk on his face. He looks ridiculously adorable that way. He's got a bottle in either hand.

"I definitely cooked. And I'm good at it. A talent I inherited from my mother. But I'll let you decide on the pre-dinner cocktails while we wait for the chicken to be done." He puts one of the bottles forward and then the other, "So, will it be rum in your mai tai or bourbon in your mint julep?"

Not being a cocktail kind of girl, I don't know which one to pick. They both sound good. And brimming with much needed alcohol. "What are you having?"

"Neither. I still have to focus hard to think like a human, so it's not a good idea to scramble my thoughts any more than necessary. But if you're looking for a recommendation, I'd say I'm partial to the mai tai."

I smile. "Okay, that's what I'll have then."

Tom disappears into the kitchen and returns with the drink. "Sorry about the lack of garnish, but while the liquor cupboard is still fully stocked the way Eunice liked it, there aren't any cherries or pineapple. I was glad to find the lime juice, though."

I take a sip and quickly decide I may become a mai tai fan. "That's fantastic!"

"Glad it hits the spot. You relax, and I'll have dinner out in a jiffy."

I do relax, finally, for what feels like the first time in a long time. It's only been a little over two weeks since Granny died and I left Dan, but those weeks have been packed with the most emotional and bizarre events of my entire life. I still don't understand how Granny was able to keep me shielded from the goings-on of her witchy life. Not to mention being an illegal importer as well as the owner of a shape-shifting house slave.

I say "house slave", but I'm pretty sure that it was something more. I mean, that box of "toys" she had upstairs and Tom's generous helping of hotness...but there's no way I'm going there and asking those questions. No way at all.

I just hope that the three of us who are in on Tom's predicament can figure out a way to get him free of it soon.

He's made roasted chicken with onions and potatoes. The potatoes are buttery and crusted with herbs, and the chicken is moist on the inside with just the right amount of crispy on the outside. He's also opened the baby carrots I bought yesterday and cooked them in a butter sauce. The food is amazing. But I think Tom will have to learn new cooking skills since a lot of the meal depends on butter, including the perfectly browned skin on the chicken. I'm tempted to pick it off, but it's one meal, right? I can go low fat again tomorrow. Yeah, I won't say anything. Why ruin a fantastic meal with a gorgeous man over a few hundred calories?

I look up from my plate, and Tom is watching me instead of eating. His messy, longish brown hair makes him look like he just got out of bed. He smiles, and I feel myself blushing like a kid and getting hot and bothered, too. Come on, Cassie, get yourself together. This isn't a date, so stop reacting like it is. The man was a cat like only a week ago.

I say, "It's all just really delicious."

"It's nothing. I wanted to say thank you for everything you've done for me." He lowers his eyes back to his meal, but I can't stop thinking about how brightly emerald green they are, and how they'd pierce my defenses if I'd bothered putting any up.

Geez, I'm having what my old Sunday School teacher would call "inappropriate thoughts" about a guy who is wearing my former cat's collar. Not to mention all the other incredibly good reasons not to be thinking of him like that.

Then suddenly, I have no trouble readjusting my attitude to something more "appropriate" as he launches off his chair to grab a spider off the wall and stick it in his mouth. I think I'm going to be sick. Okay, maybe I'm not going to be sick, but I'm definitely no longer turned on.

***

Tom doesn't come back to the dinner table. Instead, he sinks to his knees with his face in his hands and hangs his head, shaking it back and forth. I don't think he's crying, but I couldn't say for sure.

"Tom?"

"I'm so embarrassed. Even though my human side is in charge again, Cat's still a part of me. And he needs to hunt. It's who he is." Tom raises his head, and those sexy green eyes look a little crazed now.

"Would it help if you were Cat for a while? I mean, do you need to be Cat every so often? 'Cause this werecat thing you've got going on, does it have rules like that?"

"Maybe. I've almost never been human this long

at one time since..." His voice trails off and he's quiet for a moment. "Eunice kept me as Cat unless she wanted something. Even then, if she needed me to redecorate or do other manual labor, she'd shift me to Cat afterward unless she wanted me that night in bed."

I so do not want to know that last part even though I'd suspected it. But wow, not going there. I don't need to think about Gran that way when I'm still so mixed up about her. "Well, what do you think, then, if you don't know?"

"I think yes, I probably need to spend an hour or two as Cat."

"Okay. Come back to the table and finish dinner with me. Then I'll say the magic words so he can go out hunting. Because this is a great meal, with good company, and I don't want it to go to waste."

Tom comes to the table, his eyes sad, but the hungry, crazed look is gone, at least for now. They really are beautiful eyes. Oh blast. I'm turned on again.

After dinner, I tell him what a bad Tom he is, and in a moment, a sweet-faced kitten pushes his way out of the pile of Tom's clothes and purrs endearingly as he rubs the side of his face against my ankles. It's nice but weird, given my current state of horn-dogginess. Then again, he doesn't know about that. I think I'll just keep it to myself.

I walk to a downstairs window and open it wide enough for him to get out. There are sliding bolts on either side to make sure that an intruder can't lift it more than seven inches or so. That's all Cat needs to get back in. I slide the bolts in place and go into the kitchen to take care of the dishes.

Okay, so I'm adapting, right? I'm apparently a witch, and there may be a psycho warlock trying to take everything I have. Plus, my new house comes furnished with a magical werecat. And how do I know I'm taking it in stride? Because suddenly I'm daydreaming about hooking up with some guy who wears bell bottoms because he was around the first time they were cool. With nothing underneath. Because there wasn't a single pair of men's underpants in the house.

Aargh! I so did not mean to think that.

WHEN I WAKE UP, Tom is snuggled into the small of my back, sleeping soundly. I'm not sure if that's weird or not. I mean, he's a cat, but...

Well, at least sleeping with a cat snugged up against my back doesn't turn me on. I'm pretty sure it would if he was spooned up against it in human form. And now I'm thinking about snuggling against Tom in a whole other way. Note to self: I really have to stop thinking like this. I haven't even gotten over Dan yet.

Dan. Well, that helps. Now I'm sad again. I slide my feet off the side of the bed and get in a half-hearted stretch. Cat wakes up and stretches, too, his pink tongue showing through his sharp, white teeth as he yawns.

I go to the closet and grab his red robe, which I lay out for him in the hall just outside the door. He rubs against my legs and looks up at me expectantly.

Cat wanting a scratch? "Outside the room, please." He pads along obediently.

He disappears around the corner, and I say the words. "Good Tom."

After a decent interval, Tom appears in the doorway, mostly covered up in his robe, but it's open enough at the top that I'm treated to a front-row view of his man-cleavage. He says, "Thanks. I'm feeling more centered this morning. Cat needed that."

I can't stand it. Tom, despite the unstyled sixties hair, is so freaking sexy. He just is. There's something about him. How am I supposed to put up with living with him day to day when I want to pet this man until he purrs? And I'm not talking Tom the kitten here.

I manage to pull my eyes away from him and say, "You can have the shower first." He turns and walks off to the bathroom.

I go downstairs and start a pot of coffee in granny's old coffee pot. It smells amazing. I focus on that instead of my percolating lust.

Tom has to go. I have so many things to work out about what I want for my life, about Dan, about my inheritance—I don't need to deal with constant lusty thoughts about my filthy old Granny's sex slave on top of everything else.

\*\*\*

"Look, Gillian, you know what he looks like, right? And he's great. He made me this fantastic dinner the other night. Of course, he also ate a bug, which was gross. But overall, he's totally hot. I can't keep living in such close quarters with him. It's torture. I can't control what's going on inside my head." I lean on my elbows at the kitchen table in her sparkling kitchen.

Her face is a blank as she cuts into a huge pecan roll, and her tone is flat. "I can see how that could be a problem. Tom always did exude sexuality."

"Yep. My libido just pushes aside that he's been a cat and my granny's lover for over forty years. I mean, my gran's lover! Even that part where he ate a spider? Yeah, turned me off for about five minutes."

Gillian sighs. "You might as well indulge yourself. I wouldn't hold it against you, sweetheart. Well, I would just a tidge, but not for long. He's not my Tom any more."

She says it, but her words are sharp by the end. Plus, I definitely wasn't looking for her blessing.

"Gillian! That's not helping! Get jealous or something! Slap me or appeal to my common sense. I always had good common sense before this."

I think hard about how I can express what I've been thinking without my attraction to Tom getting mixed up in it, and when I think I've got it straight, I say, "The thing is, me and Tom together would almost be the same for Tom as it was with Granny Eunice—he's still trapped in the house, and

I'd control when he's a man and when he's a cat. He'd just have a nicer owner. Help me get him free of this house so he can move on."

I can see she's thinking on it, her brow furrowed. Then she says, "Have you found any handwritten books or old manuscripts? Eunice should have a grimoire or two somewhere. We all do. But to be truthful, I'm not sure I want to help. I've a good mind to leave the two of you on your own. Ever since I found out about Tom, it's been more of a sore spot than I want to admit."

"But, it wasn't Tom's fault."

"Oh bloody hell, it certainly was!" she barks.

I step back from the fury in her eyes and let her anger recede before I give her an apologetic smile and open my big mouth again.

"You're right. It was Tom's fault. And my grandmother's fault. But, Gilly, not a single bit of the fault was mine." Her face relaxes, compassion replacing anger. I try to keep the desperation out of my voice when I ask, "So, will you help? Because I'm a big, giant mess."

\*\*\*

Tom looks up, and a grin spreads across his face when he sees Gilly and I entering the parlor. He's watching TV, or, to be more exact, he's channel surfing through shows with the remote. I've noticed he does that a lot. I don't know if it's because he still has the attention span of a cat, or if it's because he has the attention span of a man. Either way, as long as he doesn't do it when I'm trying to watch something, I don't care.

He silences the TV with the power button and goes to Gillian, wrapping her in a giant hug. "It's so good to see you. Catch me up! How are you?"

"I was here two days ago. Nothing much has happened since then." She's got that wall up again.

"I know. But I haven't had many visitors over the years. I'd be more than happy to hear about every little minute of your day."

And then it hits me. How stupid am I that I didn't realize this before? How very, very lonely he must be. Knowing that, what I'm going to say won't sound very nice, but I say it anyway.

"Look Tom, you need to get out there and have a life of your own." I look to Gillian for confirmation. "I asked Gilly for help, and with a little pleading, she agreed."

Tom's shoulders drop. "I understand. Who'd want to be stuck with me? The things I've done…"

"Tom, it's not like that. It's, well, it's weird, isn't it, when I wake up and find a kitten snuggled up next to me, but later in the day, he's a fit twenty-something guy who's making me cocktails?"

"I don't mean to confuse you. Cat's a cat. He does cat things. I mean, I'm in on it, but the decisions are right for him."

I shrug. "I may be way too normal to even try to

understand that."

Gillian steps in. "Tom, let me put it another way. When you were young, you had that Jim Morrison I'll-do-what-I-want swagger, but now you're acting like you're still enslaved. And you're not. Cassie didn't take over where Eunice left off."

"I..."

"No, I'm going to finish. I hope you've learned something during your captivity about how to treat the people who love you, but even if you haven't, I don't like seeing you this way, either. The most important thing is to help you find autonomy again."

I jump back in. "Yeah, what Gilly said. That's what I meant...so until we can figure out how to remove the spell or the curse or whatever it was that put you here, there are still things you could do despite your limitations."

"Really? How? Because I can only leave as a cat."

"But I'm not stuck here," I point out. "There's no reason the two of us need to spend every waking hour cooped up in the same space. So, I'm offering you a job in the shop—for minimum wage, which should be enough to get you modern clothes and start putting together walking around money for later—and I'm going to spend more of my time away."

"A job? I accept! I know everything about the shop. I've been hanging out in it for long enough."

Gillian nods. "I said you'd like the idea. It may

not be as good a fit for your skills as cooking at the café was, but since that's not an option..."

I interrupt with the next part of the plan. "Believe it or not, Robert says he'd still be interested in having me work at the art gallery. Says I could do it part-time. And Gilly's convinced me that in the Andrewses' case, the Kevin apple fell far from the Robert tree. She says he's safe."

Tom opens his mouth to protest, but Gilly stops him. "I know why you don't like him, Tom. He was competition. That, on its own, doesn't make him evil. Robert's ambitious, but he's not his son."

Tom closes his mouth and pulls his shoulders back stiffly under her barrage.

Gillian continues, "In fact, Robert may be the only person other than Eunice who was ever able to keep Kevin under control. Which means Cassie needs him on her side. We'd be fools to think he's no longer a problem just because he's been quiet."

"Okay. It's not my decision anyway. Just don't tell everyone who I am."

"Why not?" I ask. "I mean, from what Gilly tells me, your being a magical cat-guy would be pretty normal for Giles."

Tom mumbles without looking up. "Because of what I did. All the spying. I gathered information on just about everyone in this town for Eunice, all disguised as a friendly cat."

"I think people would forgive you." I say.

Gillian puts a hand on my shoulder. "Some. Not

others. Tom may be right."

Yeah, maybe I'm naive. Around this town? No maybe about it—I'm beyond naive. "Could you be your own grandson?"

Tom looks up again. "My grandson? Not a bad idea."

"Gillian's not going to be the only person in town who recognizes you, right? And you yourself think that Robert knows who you are. So give yourself an excuse for looking like you do."

"Hmmm...so what would I call myself?" Tom asks.

"Did you have a name you wanted as a kid?"

"I did want to be Roy Rogers and ride a horse while singing cowboy songs." He looks toward Gilly and asks, "Remember?" They exchange a glance, and something intimate passes between them before he turns back to me. "Don't I look like a Roy?"

"Yeah, no...you really don't," I say. "Not at all." And, of course, I haven't got idea one who this guy Roy Rogers is, but I'm suddenly having a steamy "cowboy Tom" fantasy anyway. Geez, give my busy little brain ten seconds, and suddenly I'll never look at a bandanna the same way again. I shake it off and focus on what Tom's saying.

"Well, then, why can't I just be Tom Sanders the Third? Might as well start a family tradition."

"Brilliant," says Gillian.

Yes, brilliant. He gets more freedom, and so do I, but I know I'll still wake up mornings to find him curled up in a ball with his warm little body pressed against my back. I need a cure for that as soon as possible.

Gillian asks, "Tom, do you know where Eunice kept her grimoire?"

"Nowhere. All in here." He taps the side of his head. "She said the written word had too much power to bind to keep any records of her magic."

"It figures. But the knowledge she used to trap you can't have died with her. I'll reach out to my contacts to trace where Eunice went in Europe when she was young. Hopefully, I can locate the coven she was involved with. If the witch's grapevine doesn't yield results, there's always the Internet. Plenty of young witches are active online."

"You'd put that much work into it for me?" Tom asks softly. He looks at her with such a loving expression, I feel like I'm intruding on something personal between them and kind of want to duck out.

Gillian is matter of fact, though. It's like with that look he gives her, she slammed a fence right up in front of it. A big, brick one. With a steel overlay. "Of course. But Cassie's agreed Eunice's funds are paying for it if there are any costs involved. So, we'd both do that for you. You should have your freedom. You did something very stupid a long time ago, but you shouldn't suffer for it forever. I'll also be here every Tuesday and Thursday night after my yoga class to get Cassie started learning magic. With

Kevin still a possible danger, we'll start with protection. You'll need to stay out of the way while we work. There's nothing you can contribute."

Wow. Cold. But I am so looking forward to the magic.

THE KID FROM THE PAPER drops the Free Times into the metal distribution rack just outside the shop door. While Tom keeps his eye on the two multiply-pierced teens who are oohing and aahing over the selection of black candles and goth jewelry, I go out and grab a copy.

I can't believe what I see right on the front page. I call to Tom after the girls leave. "Hey, Tom, listen to this...'Cat's Magical Shop is a mish-mash of touristy items meant to lure passersby on their way to Salem. In Eunice Grandby's day, the shop was the stopping place of not only tourists but the rumored practitioners of black magic. Recently, Mrs. Grandby's granddaughter, Cassie Grandby, was discovered with a storeroom full of exotic items. Our source says the shop has been linked to illegal trade in traditional Asian and African medicines involving the slaughter of endangered species.

Although the Free Times has asked Miss Grandby for comment, none has been forthcoming. Summer visitors will want to avoid the premises until the legal inquiry has been completed." I look up from the paper. "I'll give him a freaking comment."

"I expect he'd dig that. Probably get it on tape and play it across the loudspeaker at the next town meeting." Tom gives a wry smile. "How many tourists read the Free Times, anyway?"

"I don't know. They've always disappeared from the rack, although I've never seen anyone take one except Natalie. She paints and picks them up in big bundles. I think she uses it as a drop cloth."

"Right on. Kevin thinks he's a much bigger fish than he is."

"You're a wise man, and I'm not going to waste time on worrying about Kreepy Kevin today. And on that note, do you mind if I wander over to the gallery? I'd love some art time. We're going to talk about when I can start."

"Go ahead. I'm ready to solo. Take as long as you want." He gives me a hug, and I pull back quickly because his body heat will have me warmed up in all the wrong places in no time if I don't. "Thanks for trusting me with this," he says.

*** 

Natalie approaches along the sidewalk with a copy of the Free Times in her hand. Behind her are a few of her friends, talking quietly to each other, expressions of concern on their faces.

"Is it true, young lady? You were caught with illegally smuggled items?"

I decide to test how much Gran's old cronies know. "Natalie, you knew Eunice. What do you think?"

"I think she could have been up to anything and that Kevin was probably in on it with her. My question is, why is he making a stink about it now? Have you rocked the boat, my girl?"

"If by 'rock the boat' you mean did I stand up to him when he broke into the shop? Did I stand up to him when he tried to manipulate me into selling up and leaving? Yes, I did those things." I look directly into each of their faces in turn, defiant, for just a moment before I say, "Anybody have anything to say about that?"

"Oh, we certainly do." Natalie raises a hand and laughs, "What is it you youngsters do? A high five? I want one of those. You do have spunk! Eunice always said you had no backbone at all. But I can see she read you wrong. You're more than welcome in this town. Do you know about our choir, dear?"

"I do now. Gilly told me your code word. And I know more about Granny Eunice than I ever wanted to, too."

"Yes, well, Eunice had her uses. She pushed back on the Andrews boys when needed, and it prevented either faction from taking total control and riding roughshod over the rest of us. She usually let others go about their business as long as no one got into hers."

"That explains a few things that I've been learning lately. I assume you needed the less shady things she stocked in the shop?"

"Oh yes, still do. And even a few things that ride along in the gray areas. Will you be keeping it open? Have you decided?"

"Yes, I have. I've even hired a new employee."

"Really? Someone from town?"

"His grandfather was, apparently. He drifted into the shop because he's been visiting the places his grandfather talked about when he was a kid. Cat's Magical Shop was one of them. He needs a job for a while, so what the heck, I hired him. Plus, you know, a generous helping of eye candy at the counter can't hurt, right?"

Wow. Those lies rolled off my tongue super easy. I'm not sure getting involved with all these secrets is such a good thing. I don't understand what Tom could have done that's so bad. I mean, it's not like he had a choice.

Natalie turns to her little band of grannies and beckons them to follow her. "Eye candy, you say? Come on, girls, I just remembered something I need to pick up at Cat's."

I should drop Tom a quick call and warn him that he's about to be the object of a bunch of elderly admiration, but I think better of it. I'm sure he would have known Natalie back in the day, and now he'll get his chance to deal with being recognized. I think he'll handle it fine. He's been doing the lying and secrets thing a lot longer than I have.

And besides, I've got a date with a wall full of east coast modern.

***

"New clothes?" I ask once I'm back at the shop, approving of the fit of Tom's new outfit. The shaggy mane prevents him looking too modern-boy, but I like the way the slim fit of the slacks accentuates his well-shaped shoulders which are now clad in a loose, white v-neck tee.

"Gillian dropped them off just after you left this morning. She says hi. Apparently, she still knows my size. Says this is what the 'young folks' are wearing these days and thinks I should try to fit in if I'm going to be in the public view. What do you think?"

I avoid telling him that I think I'd like to have him twirl for me so that I can see how the pants fit around the back. "Flattering. You look good." I nod polite approval. Inside, I applaud my own restraint.

"Good, then. I know Natalie approved, but she's not my preferred audience."

I set my packages on the counter and rest a hand on the top of the register Tom is standing behind.

"How'd that go?"

"It was strange talking to her after all these years. I feel a little dirty about knowing the things I know about her because of my spying expeditions. And I'm not sure she bought my 'Hi, I'm Tom Sanders the Third, how can I help you?' routine. Kept saying how much I look like old granddad—said she knew whose grandson I was the minute she walked in the door," Tom laughed. "And then she actually flirted with me, the randy old thing. Same old Nat. She hasn't changed much."

"Do you think we should tell her what's in her skin cream someday?"

"Nah, she hasn't needed to know to this point. And, it works, right? She definitely looks younger than seventy-five."

"Wait a minute? She's seventy-five? I thought she was the same age as Gilly, maybe younger—early sixties or something."

"The cream works."

"I guess! Maybe we should make a double batch next month and I can try it out."

"Cassie, you'll be beautiful at any age. You don't need magic potions for that."

Huh.

Not acknowledging that one. Nope. No way.

"I need to get my packages upstairs and take care of a couple other things. I'll spell you in about an hour so you can get some lunch?"

"Sure. Assuming by 'spell' you mean 'take your

place' rather than 'put you under an additional curse'?" Tom gives me a broad smile.

I giggle and give a broad smile back, then I walk upstairs and drop my day's shopping on the bed.

Beautiful? Did Tom just say he thinks I'm beautiful?.

I'D RATHER CAT CURL UP to sleep next to Cassie than prowl the night away, but he has his needs, and he won't be denied without embarrassing slips into Cat behavior during the day. When I have my druthers, I don't want to leap the counter to bat a fly out of the air in front of a tired housewife who's looking for an nonprescription form of mother's little helper.

And when I'm being completely honest with myself, I'd like to sleep curled up next to Cassie in human form. Not necessarily in a sexual way, although I wouldn't throw her out of bed for eating crackers. It's a human contact thing: I've even woken up from dreams where Eunice is holding my hand or embracing me, telling me it's okay—that she'll be back soon, and I won't be alone any longer. When I come full awake and shed the sleepy part of me that lingers with her touch for its warmth, the very idea scares the bejeebers out of me.

I get almost no contact with other people now that Cassie hardly ever gives Cat any affection. She knows the kitten is really a man, so she stays away. I'm pretty sure she'd keep me from crawling into bed with her if she wasn't asleep when I come home after the hunt.

This whole train of thought is getting to be a downer. I put the day's takings in the bag for the bank, lock up shop, and head for the back. Cassie is reading a book, waiting for the lock bag so she can walk it across the street to the night depository. I hand it to her saying, "Someday I'm going to take the deposit to the bank myself."

"You will. I know you will. Gillian and I aren't going to give up on you. Ever. She's still talking to people on the down low, trying not to draw attention. She just hasn't figured anything out yet."

"I want to believe it'll happen. I've already got more than I thought I'd ever have again by just being human most of the time, so maybe I shouldn't get greedy. The good vibes the universe is sending could end any minute." I say it like it's not important, but, like Pinocchio, what I want more than anything is to be a real boy again. It's an ache. It's hunger.

I cook us a nice dinner—nothing fancy, just good grub. We could be a couple of roommates living normal lives, doing normal things. We watch TV for a while on opposite ends of the couch, but

Cassie looks annoyed and sits up straight, then says she's going upstairs to read, when I move and my big, bare feet accidently brush over her small ones. She's kind to me, but she obviously can't stand to have me touch her. What I am, what I've done, who wouldn't be repulsed?

She turns me into Cat before she goes, and I take off outside to prowl the neighborhood for mice or even interesting shadows. But tonight, I've got a few stops planned that have nothing to do with Cat's needs.

***

First stop, the middle-striving-to-be-upper-class home of Kevin Andrews. Eunice often sent me prowling around Robert for tidbits she could keep up her sleeve in case she needed leverage, but she kept Kevin under control without my help. Now I'm keeping my eye out. I don't want any more surprises. And I don't want him anywhere near Cassie.

The windows at Kevin's house are cracked a few inches tonight to let the breeze in, and that's good for me. Not only can I see, but I'll be able to hear anyone inside. I stealthily jump to a sill and take a look. This window opens to his office. Nobody there.

I go along to the other side of the house and bingo! Kevin is sitting on the couch, shuffling through papers as he watches TV. A woman comes in with dinner on a tray. She's a cute black woman in her early thirties or so with a trim figure and a pleasant face.

After she drops off the tray, she says, "If there's nothing else tonight, Mr. Andrews, I'll be on my way home. I've got your meals all prepared and labeled with the warming instructions for this weekend." This must be the housekeeper he said he was buying headache powder for.

"Hold on for a moment, Keisha. You know I hate to have my dinner alone all the time. Have a drink with me before you go? I bought a bottle of that champagne you like."

"Sure. I don't mind. Is it in the kitchen? I'll get us each a glass."

Keisha returns from the kitchen with a champagne glass in each hand. The two of them exchange pleasantries—nothing that would indicate they are anything more than employer and employee. He doesn't slip anything into her glass. Maybe Eunice got it wrong.

"Any plans tonight?" Kevin asks.

"It's been a long week, sir. Especially with the late night tonight—but I'm not complaining. It's out of my work clothes and into a hot bath for me."

Kevin smiles. "Well, don't let me keep you from it. Here, I'll take that glass." He rises and takes the glass, then walks with her toward the back door. I jump down from the windows and haul butt to the back. "Have a good night," he calls as she walks down the back steps.

Then, only moments later, he comes out dressed in a ridiculous outfit—hooded coveralls of some kind with a mask and gloves attached. Could be what he was wearing the night of the break-in. He hustles down the street behind his housekeeper, catching up but staying a safe distance behind.

An elderly couple pass by Keisha. They nod and smile in that small town way. When they pass Kevin, they don't seem to even know he's there, although he scooted over to the far side of the sidewalk to avoid them. If they did, who wouldn't do a double-take? He looks like a bandit dressed to rob a liquor store. The coveralls even cover his shoes.

And then I realize—no one can see him but me. That's got to be why Cassie couldn't see him outside the storeroom.

Eunice's gift—the one she gave him just before she died: were the coveralls in that package? She did say her gift was "transparent." Had she made him an invisibility suit that was charmed in a way that still allowed me to track him? He would never have known that if I hadn't attacked him when he broke in to the shop. What was she planning? And how was I a part of it?

I push the thoughts away. She's six feet under now. She isn't getting out of that one. The whole coven turned out to make sure she was planted.

Whatever scheme she had in mind, I won't be a part of it now. But I do want to know what Kevin's up to.

When Keisha turns up the walk to a small cottage with a well-maintained garden, Kevin turns across the grass and goes into the backyard. He quietly closes and opens the small gate to gain entry. I slip underneath after he closes it, the bottom bar barely making an impression on Cat's tough skin as I squeeze through. Kevin goes directly to a back window. He seems to know exactly which one he wants. There's even a large, white plastic bucket hidden in the bushes next to the window which he moves and then steps up to stand on. He's been here before.

I'm too close to the ground to see what's going on inside, but a woman's shadow falls across the window, arms raised as though she's removing something over her head. Geez—the guy's got a magic invisibility suit and what he wants to do with it is spy on women while they bathe? And then I hear the zip. I no longer want to know what he's up to. I'm a small black blur as I head back to the gate.

When I was a young man, I might have chased tail all over town. I might have cheated on the wife who loved me despite my many flaws. But when Cassie changed her clothes with Cat in the room, I always made him close his eyes or look away. She thought she was alone. I had no business invading her privacy.

Men like Kevin make me ashamed to be the same species. The first thing I'm going to do when I have my humanity again? I'm going to take that bastard down.

On my way home, I stop at Kevin's homestead and make tracks across the hood of his car. Or, to be exact, across the air circulation grille. I wonder if it's difficult to get the smell of pee out of the vent system.

*** 

My next stop before the hunt is Gillian's. My angry feelings dissipate some as I get closer to her place. They're replaced by something softer and sadder.

In the small amount of time we've had to talk alone, she told me she's content. She said my disappearance left her devastated, but from that devastation came a good life. Maybe I don't want to believe her. Maybe I want to believe she has a shrine dedicated to my memory and sits in front of it every night, silent and wanting.

Forty-five years ago, I was enough of a horse's patoot to believe that. I didn't appreciate women the way they should be appreciated.

As I stalk along, distracted here and there by the scents and sounds of the night, I catch a whiff of a female in heat. Fortunately, Cat is too young to be drawn by her scent. For all I know, it's one of his children, grandchildren, or great grandchildren.

There are an abundance of black cats in this town.

Being Cat and leading a cat's romantic life has taught me one very important lesson—there's nothing fun, romantic, or exciting about running after every female who's got the whiff of seduction on her. Nothing. When you've been forced by instinct to mount every female within sniffing distance, you get to the point pretty quick where you realize mating is just mating. Cats don't have a choice. It's built into them not to be able to resist the lure. It's not conquest or an ego-stroke. It's nature insisting on it.

Humans are wired the same, but we can also make choices. If I'd chosen better, I'd be snuggled up next to my loving sixty-something year old wife, enjoying our long history spent together. I lost so much when I strayed from the woman who loved me.

What a jerk I was: I thought I was a sex-god, the poor man's Jim Morrison. Now, my chance of waking up with my beautiful, kind, smart, funny wife is as dead as that long ago rock and roll icon. And there's no going back. I learned my lesson far too late. In the past few days, I've felt anger from her, not forgiveness. But why get angry with me if she doesn't still have feelings for me?

I slink around outside her darkened house, looking for a room with a light on. I find one and jump up to the sill, hoping not to attract her attention. Gilly is sitting on a woven mat, eyes closed, sitting still in a meditation pose. Her relaxed face looks happy.

I look around the room at the pictures and knick-knacks. In many of the photos, Gillian and her husband Martin smile for the camera in a variety of exotic locations. She always loved to travel. It looks like she got to do lots of it. She looks fulfilled.

Why didn't I ever visit Gillian through those years so that I understood she'd moved on? I visited the café to see my parents until my mother died and my father sold to Robert, then passed on himself shortly after. But Gillian—after she married, maybe I didn't want to know. Why did I allow myself to believe that I could somehow be central to her life just because she and Eunice sometimes brawled about me? I can't believe that I sat there on the counter next to the cash register for years, grooming and dozing, and had the audacity to believe that anyone's universe revolved around me.

Or maybe, just maybe, not knowing helped keep me alive. What will keep me going now?

In a vacant lot just past Gillian's, I slink forward on my stomach, eyes fixed on the young mouse who hasn't heard me nor seen me where I blend into the darkness. Its whiskers twitch once, then it turns to locate the source of my predator's smell and darts away, but it's too late. I've already sprung. I play with my prey until a final bat of my paw damages something inside it beyond repair, and it stops running, stops moving, stops being what makes a mouse a mouse.

When Cat felt moved to make his toy into a token of his esteem, I went with the urge and padded along with the dead mouse dangling from my jaw, dropping it squarely in the middle of Gillian's front stoop.

If I weren't a cat, I'd smirk as I trot off, thinking of my childhood when I might have rung the doorbell and run away after having dropped off something even less desirable—now there's an idea for the next time I visit Kevin—but I think Gilly will get it, the point of this gift. Cat is giving her his thanks in his own way. He's leaving her something precious—sustenance, even if it's had all the fun smacked out of it.

Only a little later, I slip into bed and snug up against Cassie's back. I wonder how much longer she'll let me sneak in next to her warmth. I don't know what I'll do without the simple pleasure of touch. Although every cat-lover in Giles has touched Cat, most of them many times, no one but Eunice has touched me for years and years. I'd shrink from her caress but crave it at the same time. I know I went wrong years ago, but no one should ever have to know this kind of loneliness.

Cassie shifts slightly, yawning, then reaches a hand back, surfacing briefly from sleep, to run it along my spine. "Oh, there you are. Good Tom."

She didn't mean to say what she said. But intention has never counted where my magic words are concerned. She doesn't stir again as I roll away from her and hold my breath during the change, not wanting to make a sound at the pain and startle her awake. I have little control over the movements of my limbs, but I hold them as immobile as I can. Then, my cat-to-human eyes see the unremarkable shape of my meal ticket's back become the curve of a delicate shoulder in a sweetly sexy cotton nightgown with a fall of silky hair cascading over it.

The room and everything in it transforms as I transform, my human thoughts and feelings shoving to the surface as my limbs creak and strain and break their feline bonds.

When the change is done and my tortured body relaxes, I'm unwilling to leave her. I know I should go to my own room, but instead, I spoon against her gently, slipping my arm lightly across her waist. It feels good and right and human. Her warmth against my skin is arousing but also makes me protective and determined to guard her against the bad things that can happen in this town.

I'm fully awake after the shift, but I finally fall asleep by counting her precious breaths in and out, in and out, in and out instead of counting sheep.

\*\*\*

As the sun slips through the window, Cassie turns slightly and rubs a hand along my arm where it encircles her waist, patting my hand affectionately. I hold her tighter in response. Cassie's body slips from the relaxation of sleep into stiff alertness. I'm stiffly alert myself, but for an entirely different reason.

"Tom, is that you back there?"

"Yes."

"Are you wearing clothes?"

"No."

"Yeah, didn't think so. Hang on, I'll just go get your robe and toss it over my shoulder to you."

Cassie's aim is even good as she flings me my robe. I have myself respectable quickly.

"Okay, so how did that happen?"

"Me not being Cat?"

"Yeah, that."

"I got into bed, you reached back and gave me a rub, and said, 'Good Tom'."

"Oh, that's too bad." She bites her lip gently. "I kind of hoped for your sake something had changed and you could shift yourself. But you coming to my bed would be...wait a minute! You stayed in my bed afterward because?"

I go for the truth and hope she understands. "Because I wanted to be near you."

Cassie's face remains expressionless. "Oh."

I wait.

"If that ever happens again, please go to your own bed."

"You let me stay when I'm Cat. I didn't think you minded. We're the same person."

"Oh yeah, because there's no difference between a cat and a hot young guy."

"Depends on the cat." I give her what I hope is my most charming smile. She doesn't look charmed.

After a long moment, Cassie replies, "I guess it does. So, in the future, you're going to need to sleep somewhere else. Because you're right, it doesn't matter if you're Cat or not."

I try to look like it doesn't bother me, but it bothers me. It hangs like a lodestone around my neck as I make my way to the door on my huge, clunky, human feet: in the past few weeks as Cassie and I have started to know each other, the feeling of being totally alone receded for the first time in years. But it's sliding back now with a vengeance.

***

At breakfast, I tell Cassie what I observed at Kevin's house the night before.

She actually looks happy about it for a moment. "Whew. So, I wasn't seeing things. He really can make himself invisible!" Her face changes rapidly as I tell her how he's using his super power.

Then, I tell her my newly devised rock-em sock-em plan for how to use the info about Kevin to get a birth certificate for good ol' Tom Sanders the Third. Maybe I didn't think it through well enough before opening my mouth. I don't know if she's grimacing about what Kevin's done or about what I want to do.

She says, "I can see how you need a birth certificate and a new name, but I'm not sure I want to get involved with the blackmail thing. We should just call the cops. What is it with you witchy people wanting to keep it all in the family?"

"Kevin owns the cops, Cass. They're his best buddies. And it wouldn't just get me a birth certificate. It would also keep the women of this town free from that predator. Who knows where else he's peeping or what worse things he's done?"

"Yeah, but, wow—doesn't your plan seem like something Eunice would have you do?" she says.

"It's exactly something Eunice would have me do. But when you're dealing with people like Kevin and Robert, Eunice tactics are probably the only ones that work. Do you think going to the police is going to work? Robert hires the police. And Kevin—I don't know what he does to them, but he can't even get a parking ticket in this town. Believe me, every single one of them is in his pocket."

Cassie stands her ground. "I'm sure you're right, but we need to try. It's the right thing to do. Then, if they don't take the complaint seriously, I'll do what it takes. The thought that he could be looking in at me without me knowing completely creeps me out. But it just feels dirty to leverage what's happening to his housekeeper so that you can get something you want."

How in the world did this girl come from Eunice's gene pool? Out loud, I try to justify myself, but it seems lame when I hear what I have to say. "The thing about cats is they don't feel guilt. They go for what they want because that's how they're made. I've been a cat a long time. After all that time and everything Eunice made me do, maybe I've forgotten what it feels like to be human." I hang my head. "Maybe I have."

Her voice softens. "Look, I'm sorry. I didn't mean to make you feel bad. Of course I'll do what I can to get you back into the world and help out Kevin's housekeeper. I just don't know if I'd be willing to go through with making it public if Robert refused to get involved. It would be such an invasion of her privacy. From what you've said, she doesn't even know what's been happening."

"We need to make it stop either way." I shrug. "And we could post just enough of the video so that people can figure out he's making the beast with one back while looking in someone's window but not be able to tell whose window it is."

"Yeah, maybe. Gimme some time. We should talk to Gillian. She always seems to have a handle on stuff. I know you're the same age, but, no offense, Gilly is like, way more mature."

I nod, and I know she's right. When did I ever have an opportunity to gain maturity? But I'm tired of bringing Gillian in on everything. Cassie can't manage to do anything without consulting her. Then again, Eunice made all the decisions for Cassie during her summers here. Maybe she doesn't have much experience making them on her own. Who knows what her fiancé was like. He might have been just as controlling.

GILLIAN TAKES A SEAT in the kitchenette and gives me a smile as I hand her a cup of tea the way she likes it—two sugars and a teaspoon of cream. Cassie sits opposite her in the only other chair, and I lean against the counter, waiting for the announcement Gilly said she had to make.

"I'm leaving for France tomorrow. I remembered something Eunice told me years ago about her coven there. Her high priestess was a woman named Madame Aurelle. Eunice said she was the most powerful witch she'd ever known. I was able to track down the coven through some of my sources who contacted their sources, and so on. My thought is that someone may know the secret of the magic that bound Tom as a cat. If they do, maybe they'll know how to undo it. But they're certainly not going to discuss that kind of magic with me through email."

"Gillian, that's fantastic!" Cassie says.

I walk Gillian to the door and give her a hug on her way out. "Thanks for everything you're doing. You're still the best, baby."

"Baby? Really?" She calls back to Cassie. "While I'm gone, please explain to Tom why calling a full-grown woman 'baby' makes him a caveman."

Then she's gone, and our trio is a duo.

Back in the kitchen, Cassie turns to me and smiles weakly. "Truthfully, I don't mind being called baby. Dan did it all the time."

She bustles off up to her room. Cassie's with Dan now, at least in her head. Gilly's gone to France. Tom is alone.

***

A day later, I'm glad Cassie didn't mention my plan to Gillian. I think she'd have rousted it pretty quick. Instead, we get to go forward with it. It gives me something to focus on other than Cassie's skittishness with me.

Sure, I took a leaf from Eunice's book to design the plan, but in this case it's justified. If things go well, Kevin won't be wandering around the shop eyeing up Cassie's merchandise any more.

I've always been good with my hands, although it does take a few hours for the muscle memory to come back after I've spent time as Cat. I fashion a harness with a pocket for Cassie's cell phone out of a piece of old wire I find in the storeroom, then

Cassie says the words so Cat can try it on.

After I've shifted and am mobile again, she attaches the harness to my collar after slipping her phone into it. They do amazing things with electronics these days. I'm still not sure I believe there's an entire computer in that tiny thing. I'm glad when she can't resist scratching my ears, but she catches herself and pulls away quickly. She must be so repelled by what I am.

She presses the button for the camera, and I slowly circle the room, making sure to jump up like I would need to when getting up to the sill at Kevin's house.

We review the tape later, and while my ability to point the camera in the right direction isn't perfect, it does the job. When I tried to get Cassie in the middle of the frame and follow her as she walked across the room, I only lost her twice and quickly got her back into the picture.

With practice, this is going to go okay. We decide to try it out later tonight on the real target.

\*\*\*

I return with the video, and Cassie carefully removes the collar from around my neck, lays my robe near me, and says, "Good Tom," as she walks out of the room.

When I'm presentable, I join her at the table while she watches through the video. There's nothing to see but Kevin sitting and reading, getting up for a cup of tea, and waving distractedly at Keisha as she announces she's leaving at the end of her shift. The camera veered crazily side to side for a moment when I jumped from the window ledge and pushed my way through the bushes to film Keisha walking home, but it did show that the setup would work. I wish I'd gotten something on him, but I can be patient until he takes a wrong step again.

When she's done watching, Cassie looks up and says, "Okay, that was weird to watch. Voyeur much? I think we should just go to the cops without proof."

"You know we can't. Maybe not even with proof. It's not like I want to watch it happen again, but when you've been sent to spy as many times as I have, it becomes second nature. Anyway, Cat isn't judgmental. He just watches and waits for his opening to turn the situation to his advantage."

"Why do you always say 'Cat' like it has a capital c and is like...somebody else?"

"Cat is somebody else. Or a separate being, at least."

"But how?" she presses. She obviously isn't letting me go on this one.

"Like I could explain the freaky existential trip I'm on? Because I can't. Not so it makes any sense. I experience Cat's feelings and needs and ways of processing information, and I'm pretty sure Cat's consciousness experiences mine: it's anyone's guess what a cat makes of that. Our bodies share the same space, but the only time both bodies are physically present at the same time is during the shift. I don't know how it works, but we're two beings sharing the same space, bodies, and consciousness. Cat's inside my head, and I'm inside his body."

Cassie's forehead wrinkles as she takes it in. She gives me a wry look and asks, "Which one of you is the one who crawls into bed with me?"

"Both of us. Cat for warmth. Me for a different warmth. A human kind of warmth."

"I'm so sorry. I don't even know what to say..." A tear glistens at the corner of her right eye. She blinks it back.

"Look, don't say anything." I take a deep breath. "But, because we're talking about it, and we might not do that again, I've got to come clean on one thing. Just try not to judge me until you've heard me out. It could change the way you think of me."

Cassie nods her head, but her brow furrows slightly, and she's biting her lip on one side.

"Between Eunice and me...I tried to put as much of a barrier against her as I could, but Cat had no problem with her. Cat never saw himself as anything but independent, doing what cats do. He kept me alive, because if I'd had to accept as a man the things that were expected of me..."

I hang my head, but there's no extra courage waiting at my feet. I raise it again. Her eyes never left me. "What I'm trying to say is—I seldom fought Eunice on any of it. Very early, I did. I was angry—angry about what she did to me, to Gillian, but in the end, I accepted the relationship with her that cats have with their masters and mistresses—distant but dependent, and trading my affection and skills for food, shelter, and life. Based on what I've seen spying on people all these years, a lot of people live their lives that way."

I take a deep breath before I continue. "I'm not a good man, Cassie, although I'm a pretty good cat."

I can't bear to look at her for even a second longer, and I look away, recalling all the rotten things I've done over the years without complaint, knowing that anyone with self-respect would have fought it, accepted death if that was the alternative. But I couldn't get rid of the hope. It was the one thing I had that I could call my own.

Cassie is up and moving around the table, her arms stretching out to pull me to her. My head rests on her shoulder, and her breath warms my forehead. She murmurs something into my hair, but I can't hear the words. I place my arms around her waist and she holds me for a long time.

When we finally let go of each other, somewhere deep inside where I've stored up all the

rage, a spark of healing springs toward the light. This girl, this amazing girl, just keeps forgiving me.

THE GOOD NEWS IS that cats don't get bored. They can't hold information long enough to find the next round of the same thing repetitive. The bad news is that I do.

Day three of Kevin-watch and still there's nothing going on. I begin to think that I dreamed it all up. I have endless images of Kevin watching TV, reading papers, or eating dinner. I have lots of time devoted to pretty Keisha's cooking and serving. What I don't have is anything that points a finger at Kevin as the devil I know he is.

Cat's eyes start to close. He's been pushing for a nap for an hour now, but I've been fighting him to stay awake.

Then, Keisha comes out of the kitchen, drying her hands on a checked hand towel after washing the dinner dishes, and Kevin waves her over when she tells him she's ready to take off for the night.

"Have a glass of wine with me before you go? I'm celebrating a new business acquisition, and it's no fun celebrating alone."

"Sure, Mr. Andrews. You know I don't mind a glass of wine. Thanks." She folds the towel as she walks to the couch and lays it across her legs when she sits in the chair kitty-corner to Kevin and reaches for the glass he offers. She communicates with nods, an occasional smile, and noncommittal responses to his small talk. She's obviously tired, but it's also clear she doesn't want to upset her employer.

When Kevin finally walks her to the door, I wait outside to see if he's going to follow her. Bingo! Tonight's the night.

I got every second of it. Even the Kevie-porn. I'll make sure Cassie's warned about that, though. I don't need her to be even more skittish around me.

It doesn't take long before he zips back up. I figure he'll head back to his place, but he goes in the direction of downtown instead. It's quite a haul—a mile at least, but I guess if he's planning on not being spotted, he can't drive.

I feel like I'm going to cough up a fur ball, if not my entire digestive system, when I realize where he's heading.

*** 

It's become our ritual over the last few days. I go

in through the open downstairs window, Cassie removes the harness and shifts me, and then we stand close together watching the video as we review what I've got.

Not tonight, though. I come in through the back and slink behind the furniture, careful to make sure I can't be seen from the side window where I know Kevin lurks. I sit directly below it and meow to get Cassie's attention.

She looks over casually, a question in her eyes, and I do my best to signal her by widening mine and shaking my head up and down. We really need to get some signals going for these need-to-communicate-with-a-cat situations. She turns back to her book and says "Good Tom", careful to keep her eyes averted.

I force myself to stay silent as the transformation takes place. Then I blast up, slam the window open and see no one there, but my right fist smashes into where I think Kevin's face should be. The result is a scream and a satisfying crunch and the sound of footfalls running away.

"Stay away from us, you animal!" I yell after him, no longer sure where he is because apparently only Cat can see him, but I think he's probably long gone. Just to be confident I'm right, I turn quickly to Cass and say, "Shift me."

When I leap to the sill, he's nowhere to be seen.

"Was he?" Cassie looks terrified. She says the words to make me a man again. She forgets to turn away for modesty's sake. I grab her in my arms and comfort her. Then, she suddenly pushes away.

"Ummm…you, we…clothes, Tom. Please."

I make myself decent and rejoin her in the living room. It seems wrong to feel triumph as I watch the scenes I captured, this time with all of the colors represented through my human eyes. I feel a sadness for Keisha I didn't feel as Cat. His influence on me fades more every day now that I'm mostly human. But that's a double-edged sword. I'm not used to the strength of human emotions any more.

"Well, looks like we've got him. Now all we have to do is go to the cops with it," Cassie says.

"Are we going to wait for Gillian for that?"

"No. I'm calling them tomorrow. There's evidence now. No reason to put it off any longer." I know she's right, but I worry for her. This time, I almost wish she would wait.

She asks, "Are you hunting tonight?"

"No, how could I? I don't feel like you'll be safe."

"Oh, I'll be safe. I'm going to lock all the doors, go upstairs, and throw a big old protection net around this house with the spells that Gillian's taught me. I'd like to see him get even a toe into the house tonight without losing it."

"You're sure?"

"Yeah, I'm sure. I'm calm now, and I know how Cat needs to hunt when something awful happens."

I don't tell her it's me that needs it, that every

nerve in my body is jittering with the emotions I don't know how to handle. When I'm riding inside Cat again, I escape into the night without my harness, free of human responsibilities.

Cat is still too young to be a danger to much of anything in this reincarnation, but just pouncing at shadows takes the edge off the hunting instinct. I love the smell of danger, but I hope I haven't landed Cassie right in it.

***

The big cop accepts the muffin Cassie offers and takes a hearty bite that he washes down with coffee. I watch from the armchair through Cat's eyes as Cassie tells him why she called the station. We decided it would be better coming from her without "Tom the Third" around. He's still the new guy in town and his identity won't hold up to much scrutiny. We also decided it would be a smart idea not to mention the film until we see the way the wind blows.

When Cassie says Kevin's name, it's like a curtain drops across the officer's face. It goes hard and blank almost on cue. Before she's even done with her story, he says, "So you're saying that one of this town's most respected citizens is pulling a peeping Tom on his employee on a regular basis, but she hasn't bothered to come forward? And why should I believe this?"

"I just think you should look into it. You know, stake the place out or something. See for yourself."

He gets up and stands over her, menacing. His stone face has threat written all over it. "Here's what I think is going on. The snotty little granddaughter of Eunice Grandby, who sold smuggled items right here on these premises, decides she doesn't like what the local paper printed about it. She thinks it's a good idea to go after the owner of that paper with an ugly story for some payback. So, listen up: Mr. Andrews won't put up with it, and I won't put up with it. Don't bother calling the department for anything again. We won't be stopping in to listen to your lies."

The cop turns to leave, grabbing another muffin from the counter on his way by. He suddenly turns back, the expression on his face softening, and looks at her strangely, as if he's forgotten something.

Well, I guess we know which way the wind blows. I get to a sitting position, ready if Cassie needs to shift me to help her out against the brute. She agreed she would if she had to, but I pressed her hard to get that promise. I only hope she follows through and doesn't depend on her newly developed magic skills. I don't like this guy lording it over her. I'd like to get a few licks in.

But after a tense minute, the cop turns and leaves quietly. And that's the end of it. Except for the part where Cassie starts sniffling. To her credit, she shrugs it off quicker than I thought she would. Two weeks ago she would have been sobbing her head off.

I don't say I warned her, but I did. I told her Kevin was buddies with them all. We'll need to be extra vigilant now.

***

That night when Cassie leaves to walk the day's takings to the bank, Kevin stops her across the street from the shop, dragging her into the narrow alley next to the bakery, his hand over her mouth. She tries to break away from him, and he moves in, threatening, his body too close to hers, his eyes narrowed, his mouth tight and angry.

I run from the behind the counter to the door and burst onto the sidewalk, leaving a pile of clothes behind as my body folds into itself. I don't even glance down the sidewalk to see if there's anyone else around. I don't care who sees.

Damn it! Where did this traffic come from? Cat blasts across the asphalt as soon as the moving cars have traveled on.

But she's alone now, sobbing. He's already skulked out of the back of the alley.

She tells me what happened between gasps that escape as she works to get back under control, clinging to Cat, her tears rolling off his fur where she holds him tight against her shoulder. "He said…he could have me…right here…right on the sidewalk...and not a single cop would move to stop him."

I'm going to kill that bastard.

***

Until I can kill him, I need to make sure Kevin's staying put far away from the shop. After dinner, I tell Cassie I want to film him again, but it's a ruse. What I want is to case the joint for when I'm fully human and can make sure he never frightens her again. I know what he's capable of. I know what he did to Eunice, even if I can't prove it. He deserves to be put down for the rabid dog he is.

It's dusk when I jump to the sill at Kevin's house and my feet slip before they find purchase. The harness adds just enough weight to keep me unsure in gauging my movements. But it's okay; I catch myself with Cat's sharp claws and make only the slightest noise as I start to pull myself up.

I'm too intent on my efforts, too recently reincarnated as Cat for my senses to be finely tuned. I scrabble for a firm hold on the sill and don't notice what's going on inside the house. The screen pops out of the window, and Kevin has me by the scruff of the neck before I realize what's happening and can let go to drop back into the bushes.

I claw and I bite, but a small cat is no match for a grown man.

I hope Cassie isn't too sad when I never come

home.

Kevin carries me to the kitchen, careful to hold me out at arm's length to keep himself safe from my claws. He's got a fading purple-black bruise under his right eye. I'm pleased to see I've done him damage even though I'm helpless now. He blats away about his evil plans for me, for Cassie, for the town. Then he opens a cupboard door with one hand and takes out a brown dropper bottle.

He moves his hand around the back of my head and forces a finger in at the side of my jaw. It pries my mouth open slightly but doesn't put his fingers in danger from my teeth. Once he's got me immobilized, hanging in the air from one of his soft, feminine hands with my eyes and mouth wide open, he holds the dropper above my mouth and gives a squeeze. I try not to swallow.

It goes dark slowly, but at least there is no pain.

I TAKE ONE OF GRANNY'S pre-mixed anti-anxiety herbal mixes after dinner, and while I'm alert, I'm able to focus on something other than my worries. I'd used it before big games when I was a kid, and it always did the trick. If life keeps up like it has, I'm going to need a ton of it. Fortunately, I'll be able to make it because while Granny didn't leave a grimoire, she did leave the recipe book for the herbal stuff we sold in the shop. Everything the shop sells is in there including the magical phrases that I always thought were just Granny's eccentricity, but there's nothing other than that. Nothing that would help Tom.

My book is engrossing, and I don't realize it's after midnight. Tom should be home by now. He wouldn't have gone hunting with the harness on. It restricts his movements too much. He would have come home to have it removed before he went back out for the night.

I want to tell him the good news: Gillian emailed today, and she's found the coven Granny joined when she was in France, in a place called Côte-Louanne, which she says is an awful lot like a French version of Giles. She's invited for dinner with the old high priestess, so she hopes she can find something out about Granny's time there. I suppose I can hold onto the news if Tom's still prowling—it'll be just as exciting tomorrow. And I've put a protection net spell up around the house, so I don't need to worry about Kevin. I hope. It won't be as strong as one of Gilly's, but it should get me through the night. Still, I'd feel more secure with Tom here. Maybe I shouldn't have urged him to go.

By half past one, I'm not able to make myself believe that he's still gone because he's doing something fun. I'm stressed despite the concoction I took earlier. I'm looking up from my book every couple of minutes, no longer knowing or caring what it's about. I need to see him slinking into the room satisfied and leap onto the bed, and every time I think I hear or sense movement and look up, another grain of worry drops into the pile because he's not there. I pour a glass of boxed wine in hopes it will help me relax, and it works a little, but the anxiety has gotten hold of me now, and I can't push back the image of Cat crushed under the wheels of a car or torn apart by a raccoon. Then again, that wouldn't put an end to Tom—he'd shift, then regenerate as Cat, wouldn't he? Like he did that night Kevin broke into the shop. Except there was also something about him having only nine lives? I think he told me that.

An hour later, I realize that my staying up isn't going to bring him through that window any sooner. I finish a second glass of wine with more anxiety-soothing powder and take myself up to bed, hoping to wake to a black ball of fur butting me with its head so I can turn it back into a man.

\*\*\*

In the morning, after a crappy night's sleep, I hurry down the hall to Tom's room. He's not there. My heart hurts and my stomach clenches. I go downstairs, hoping to find him crashed out in the shop window or on the counter or sleeping on a parlor chair, but he's nowhere to be found.

I eat my solitary breakfast, shower, dress, and spend the morning prowling around downtown, looking under porches, and exploring all the nooks and crannies up and down the street for a small black cat before I open the shop. No one comes in for an hour, giving me plenty of time to let my imagination run wild about where Tom might be.

It figures that my first visitor is Kevin. Ever since I learned how truly vile he is, he's almost become a cartoon villain to me with his comb-over and general smarminess. He wouldn't try anything in the shop, would he? I didn't have time to put up another protection spell this morning, but my bat is still under the counter. Maybe he'd like a taste of that again.

"Dear Cassie. I had a visitor last night. It was quite late, and I was concerned for him—your sweet little kitten, what's his name, again?"

I nearly stop breathing, but I force myself back under control. "Just Cat. Like the shop."

"Well, 'just Cat' was prowling around in my bushes, and I tried to catch him because he looked like he'd gotten something caught around his neck, but no—he was far too clever for me and eluded me. I do hope he got home all right?"

I'm quaking inside, seriously quaking, but I don't let him see that. "He's not back yet, but he sometimes doesn't come home right away in the morning." I'm desperate trying to read his expression to figure out the true reason for his visit.

His tight smile doesn't waver as he says, "Oh my, are you thinking of our talk in the alley? And our unpleasant conflict over Eunice's secret stock? There are always losers and winners in business. It can be cut-throat, even in a sleepy little town like Giles. But I've put that unpleasantness behind me. I hope that you can, too."

I just stand there looking at him, appalled that he thinks of everything that's happened between us as a bad business deal.

"Oh well, in time, perhaps. I do hope you find

your sweet little Cat. They say that cats have nine lives, don't they? I hope the poor thing's time isn't up."

As he leaves, I have an overwhelming urge to take another shower. And I'm sick with worry about Tom now. I toss the rest of my anti-anxiety powder into the trash. No point in drugging myself. This isn't my imagination running away with me. Tom's in trouble.

I grab my cell and find the contact for Gillian. When she picks up, I don't bother with hellos or pleasantries, I just blurt it out, "Tom's missing. I'm afraid Kevin did something to him. I don't know what to do."

"First, take a breath. Then tell me why you think Kevin did something."

I relate the story of Kevin's visit as Gillian murmurs here and there to indicate she's listening.

"It sounds like you're right to be concerned. However, my dinner with Aurelle Louvelle and her granddaughter, Aurelie, is tonight, and I can't leave yet. With luck, I'll get enough information and can arrange a flight back right after."

"I could use you here right now, Gilly. I feel so alone. I didn't realize how much I'd come to expect him to be here."

Gilly reassures me, and I feel better listening to her soothing voice.

"You need to go to Natalie and enlist the coven's help. They should be able to invoke a location spell to help you find him."

"Are you sure I can trust Natalie?"

"Probably. She definitely has a hatful of hate for Robert and Kevin Andrews. If she could help you do something to spite them, she'd do it gleefully."

"But Tom wouldn't like it. It feels like I'd be betraying his secret."

"I'm sure Nat has sussed Tom out already. She's not a stupid woman by any means, and she's the most powerful witch in the coven now that Eunice is gone. If anyone can help with this until I get back, it's Nat."

We hang up, but my head is still working on what Gillian said. I don't want to admit that I'm desperate with fear for Tom. I don't want the strange life we've shared together for the past few weeks to end. I don't know if he's my cat or my friend, or just a guy I lust after in a weird, furry sort of way. I pick up the phone and call the number she gave me, but there's no answer. I don't want to leave a message, but I do it anyway. It's just a request to call. I can't give her the details this way.

I know he'll be back soon. I know it.

IT'S DAY TWO BREAKFAST without Tom now, and Natalie hasn't returned my call. I get up early and search again under every porch in town as soon as the sun comes up. I hang up lost cat posters. Big reward. Have you seen him?

I stop back at the house at noon and grab some lunch, try to call Natalie but end up leaving a message again that I need to talk to her. I can't tell her what it's about in a message. Anyone could listen to it if she's got an old skool answering machine like Gran's. I'm not sure I trust Natalie, but I know I don't trust any random stranger who might hear a message playing because they're hanging out when she picks it up. And she barely even knows me. Why would she jump if I tell her I need to talk?

I decide it's time to find out where she lives and take this bull by its horns. Her address is in the phone book, so I drive to the east end of town where she lives.

Just as Natalie answers the door, my cell rings. I pick up, and Natalie waits with one hand poised, ready to close the door. I get the feeling she's not the most patient woman.

It's Gillian. "I'll be home tomorrow night. We have a lot to talk about. I've got what we're looking for."

My spirits lift, and then I remember that whatever she's got, we have to find Tom before it can help him. I'm not a praying woman, but I'm pulling at the universe to get behind me on this one.

Nat's still looking at me, but her hand is already pushing the door forward. I shove the phone at her. "It's Gillian."

Nat's eyes grow big as she listens to Gilly talk and ushers me into the house.

*** 

Gillian folds me in a big embrace. "Has there been any news about Tom?"

"No, nothing. I'm crazy worried at this point. Natalie's gathered the coven like you asked. I don't know that I trust them, but something has to happen."

Gillian turns and charges along, following the arrows toward the baggage claim. "Assuming Tom is alive and not being actively hidden from magical forces, the coven should be able to find him. Are you sure Robert isn't involved in this? I doubt he would be, but..."

"No, I'm not sure about anything. How could I be? Kevin didn't actually say he'd done anything. He just hinted, but it made my skin crawl."

"If Robert's involved, he'd be able to hide Tom from a spell, but Kevin doesn't have that kind of casting power. He's more nearly a pharmacist than a warlock."

Gillian fills me in on what she found out while I drive as quickly homeward as I can without killing both of us. "Apparently, shape-shifting was all the rage back in the middle ages in Europe. Members of the coven where Eunice was a novice continue the practice. Witches become one with their animal partners to honor nature, not to control it."

"So, like werewolves? That kind of thing?"

"Werewolves, werebears—wererabbits, if someone's inclined that way. It seems the myths are mostly wrong, but like all myths, they gained power as they were told and retold. The joining is chosen by the witch and requested of the Goddess in a sacred ceremony. Eunice participated in one of those ceremonies with the coven and must have gained the knowledge that way. Except she corrupted the magic for her own uses."

I keep my eyes on the road, but I want to stop and pull all the information out of her. "Corrupted it how?"

"Aurelle said she must have forced Tom to participate in the ritual without his consent, much as she taught you magic without you being aware of it. And to be successful, she had to mix in other magic to bind his power and allows words spoken by another to activate the spell. What do you young people call it? A mashup, right? None of that is part of the original magic. The high priestess is going to talk to anyone who remembers Eunice to see if there are rituals they can think of that Eunice might have learned to create the spell."

"So, you don't really have an answer?" The excitement that was fueling my optimism fades.

"Not yet, sweetheart, but we do have another puzzle to solve that might help."

"Another one?"

"The high priestess believes that when Eunice died, no one else should have been able to make Tom transform. She doesn't understand how you have that power. She wants me to see if I can shift him, because if I can't, there may be something even darker going on here."

"What does that mean?"

Gillian shrugged. "We'll cross that bridge when we come to it, pet. Just trust me for now and let's focus on finding Tom. None of this has any value if we can't locate him."

She obviously isn't going any further with whatever she hinted at, so I let it drop. At least she's back and convinced that we'll not only find Tom, but she'll be able to help him with his problem, too.

\*\*\*

When we get back to the shop, six sleepy members of the coven are sipping tea in Granny's downstairs parlor. I hear Natalie rummaging in the kitchen. Although Gillian says Nat likes to take off with other people's good silver, somebody had to make the tea, and I can't worry about anything as meaningless as tableware right now, anyway.

She assures me that with the two of us and Nat, nine can also be a powerful number. She certainly doesn't want Kevin or Robert participating and there are a few other coven members she believes were loyal to Eunice. It's feels so normal and civilized as Natalie comes out of the kitchen with a tray of cheese, crackers, and cookies.

After she plops the tray on the coffee table for people to serve themselves and takes her own seat, Natalie dips a cookie into her tea and says, "Well, Gillian, begin."

Gillian nods and looks to the group. "I need your help. Or more appropriately, my ex-husband Tom needs the coven's help."

Natalie butts in when Gillian pauses. "Most of you knew his grandson was visiting and working in the shop." She cocks an eyebrow, her expression bemused. "But couldn't you just swear after meeting him that Tom Sanders the original had simply been using Eunice's creams to good effect all these years? Because that young man could tell me that he's Tom Sanders' grandson until the cows come home, but I recognized that tight little tush when I saw it. Tom himself has been working the counter." All the eyes in the parlor turn back expectantly toward Gillian.

"Yes," Gillian says. Most of the guests look surprised.

"You've also seen him in the shop every time you visited over the past forty years, because he's been trapped as Cat since he supposedly left town," I say from where I stand behind Gillian.

This time, there are absolutely startled looks, and one long gasp.

Gillian steps back in. "Cassie discovered the secret when there was a break-in at the shop. Cat was badly injured, and when he died, Tom was revealed. Unfortunately, he quickly returned to cat form."

I'm glad Gillian doesn't tell everyone how badly I reacted when I first met Tom.

She continues. "We've made progress by giving Tom his human form for long periods of time, but now he's disappeared. We think he may be in trouble, and we need help finding him. We'd like to ask for help performing a location ritual with as much oomph behind it as this group can muster."

Voices come from all around:

"Of course, we'll help...."

"We can start right now..."

"I've got a map in the car...I'll go get it."

"Does anyone have a silver medallion with them?"

"Can you believe it? Tom back after all these years?"

It's heart-warming seeing all these people jump in to help. I think Tom would be surprised to know how eager people are to make things better for him. I look around as people start to move to get maps and medallions and to talk to Gillian about what's needed, and I feel the tears coming on. Maybe, just maybe, I'll see Tom again.

AT NIGHT, IN THE WOODS, dressed in black robes, these ordinary looking people take on the look of the extraordinary. I can hardly believe I'm here. My neck and shoulders ache from the tension of wondering what comes next. I could have stayed home while the coven worked their hoodoo-voodoo, but if this is what it takes to save Tom, I'll be a freaking witch just like my Granny wanted.

I've got a robe, a gift from Eunice's closet, over my capris and t-shirt. I've also got a dropper jar of rosemary oil from the shop. Gillian says we'll need it. She assures me that as long as I follow the lead of the others, I can't mess anything up. I better not. Because my heart is beating so rapidly I'm still not sure I won't just cut and run if anything too eerie happens. This isn't like our Tuesday and Thursday sessions. This is serious magic.

Setting up the ritual is done quietly: everyone

discussed their role before we left the house, and everyone knows what they need to do. Gillian and Jane set out a series of nine candles in a circle around the map, which Natalie has already placed at the center of the ritual grounds. I put a drop of rosemary on the base of each one. Once they're in place, we line up behind them, one person each to a candle, and wait for Natalie to nod. Then we pass a lit taper around the circle to light them up. In the silence, I can almost hear my heart still beating too fast.

Gillian, as the person closest to Tom for the longest period of time, begins a chant, and on the second repetition, others start to chant with her. At each repetition more and more join in, until we're chanting the words of the spell in one voice. Even me—I'm chanting as one with them, and as I do, my fear begins to ease away.

Gillian raises the silver pendant—a replica of a knife—she's been holding, and it hangs straight down, not moving. Then it begins to tilt inward slightly under its own power, toward the map and away from gravity. As our chant grows more urgent, the medallion continues to lift until it's floating out at an angle on its chain, the tip of the small blade pointing to the map. At the end of the next round, Gillian lets go of the chain and the pendant shoots to the map in an unwavering line, piercing the paper when it hits and sticking through the map into the dirt below.

With solemn grace, Gillian goes to the map and removes the marker. Then she says, "I'll be damned. He's at the pound."

I'm going to kill that bastard.

\*\*\*

Gillian and I arrive at the pound on the edge of the town at least an hour before it opens. We want to make sure they don't have time to get started culling for the day. Operated by the county, it's a small, old, badly maintained building that smells of urine, feces, and decay.

There's a worker dressed in stained coveralls behind the counter, but when I try the door, it's still locked. Well, that's not stopping me today. I focus on the place at the base of my spine where Gillian says magic lives, and position my hand over the doorknob, willing it to move. A single, small blue spark leaps from a fingertip. It's enough. When I try again, the knob turns, and I head for the worker behind the counter.

"You've got my cat, and I want him now!"

"Look, sister, we're not open yet. You can wait outside," he says.

I'm ready to tear the place apart to get Tom out of there, but I keep it under control. The people who work here don't know what they have. Why would they? He's just another stray cat.

"Not good enough. He's a black kitten. Green

eyes. He's mine, and I want him. So you're open for the day. Now."

He stands there for a minute, probably trying to decide how crazy I am. Apparently deciding it might not be worth the risk, he says, "Dang, keep yer hair on, lady. He's back here." Gillian and I follow behind him as he hooks a key off the wall and opens the door into the back.

When we reach Tom's cage and the workman opens the cage door for me to gently pick up the sleeping Cat, I'm barely bothered by the stench of urine and stale dog food. As far as I'm concerned it's the most amazing smell in the world, because it's brought Tom back to me.

I hold him close, rubbing my cheek against his soft fur, and he opens his eyes. I can hardly wait to get him home so that I can tell him what a good Tom he is.

CASSIE CLASPS ME to her chest, nuzzling me with her cheek as she carries me to the car. Even Gillian is tutting and cooing at me. I think they're glad to see me.

I've never been so happy in my life to see anyone as I am to see my two girls. And as soon as I'm able, I'm going to get even with Kevin. I'd like to see anyone try to stop me.

As I counted down the days in there, I was sure I'll end up a victim of their animal Auschwitz. If Cat had died in one of their chambers, no one would have seen me as I shifted. My human body would have succumbed to the gas soon after, crammed into a cage only big enough for a large dog. Even if I'd gotten another life, that one would go, too, pretty quick. I wonder how they'd have explained it if it was a man they removed from their gas chamber and not a cat.

When we get home, Cassie and Gillian politely turn their backs while Cassie says the words that make me human.

I let them know I'm respectable again once I've hurried into the clothes that were laid out for me. Both of them rush into my arms. A tear glistens at the corner of Gillian's eye—she's stopped being angry now, I know she has—but Cassie is openly sobbing. I want to join them out of sheer relief, but I don't cry; the best I can manage is a little mist. I didn't cry much before I was made Cat, but with Cat's influence, I haven't shed a real tear in years. Cats don't have the requisite emotions. I wonder if I'll ever have the ability again.

When we release each other, Gillian finally asks, "Tom, how did you end up in the pound?"

"Kevin caught me outside his window. When I woke up in a cage in the car, he told me that he had a pretty good idea of who I am—he knew I was Tom, at least. I think he's had some conversations with Robert on the subject."

"Why did he take you to the pound? Why didn't he just kill you himself?"

"Strangely enough, he didn't let me in on that part of the plan. My best guess is he didn't want to deal with what would happen if I shift when Cat dies. He has a good reason to suspect I would. Then he'd have a big, strong man to deal with instead of a defenseless cat. I don't think ol' Kevie has the courage to face a man. Plus, a man's body is a much bigger problem to dispose of. They use a gas chamber at the pound. I guess he figured that even if I shifted after Cat died, I'd be shifting into a poisoned environment. Their problem to deal with, I suppose."

Cassie reddens with anger. "I swear I'm going to kill him. I swear it."

I take her hand and hold it gently between both of mine to calm her. It feels good there. Right.

"I appreciate the sentiment, Cass, but I had a lot time to think, and he's not worth getting bent out of shape about. I thought he was, but that's what put me in the pound. I may be mostly cat, but my life, such as it is, is worth way more than his will ever be. And yours? Priceless. Never, ever risk yourself for me."

She gives me a look I can't interpret. Something's hidden in there behind her anger at Kevin, if only I could understand what it is. I continue. "We still have the original tape, so let's just talk to Robert now, before it gets any more out of hand. Kevin didn't mention him once while he bragged about his exploits. I'm beginning to believe Robert may not even know what his son's been up to. Plus, I think if he finds out, he's more than capable of reining Kevin in."

Gillian holds up her phone. "Dialing him now." She walks into the hall with the phone to her ear.

"That's taken care of," Gillian says, walking back

into the sitting room. I'm still holding Cassie's hand, but Gillian's return makes me feel awkward, like I'm betraying her by hanging on to Cassie for too long. I let go.

"Get your video backed up before he gets here," Gillian tells Cassie. "You want to make sure he can't destroy your only copy if he manages to get it away from you."

"Already taken care of," Cassie says. Kevin's got the phone now, but the video was always in the cloud.

"And...Tom, you look like you just got caught with your hand in the cookie jar. Did I interrupt a moment there?"

Cassie flushes slightly. I look to my feet, not really sure what to say.

"Yes? No? Because I don't care. If you're worried that I do, you're at least thirty years too late for me to be able to work up any jealousy. I divorced you, I've forgiven you, and that's that." I look for any sign that she's hiding her feelings for me, but she's telling the truth. She may not be angry any more, but she's not holding a torch for me, either. Still, how could there be a moment? I'm years older than Cassie, no matter what I look like. And I know she can't cope with what I am, the thing that I am.

"Just celebration and friendship," I say. I look to Cassie, but she's conspicuously looking everywhere but at me. Does that mean something?

Gillian's phone chimes. After she glances at the

screen, she says, "I need to get this. France," and she's off again to the hall.

I sit on the couch. Cassie sits, too, in the big armchair, looking across at me.

"Did you feel like that was a 'moment', like Gillian said?"

"Um..uh...you mean between you and me?"

"Yes, I'm pretty sure that's what I'm talking about. Was there someone in the room I didn't notice?"

She looks flustered again. "Don't be an ass. I'm not comfortable with this conversation."

"But you missed me? In that way?"

"Yeah, well...who wouldn't want a boyfriend who's exactly like a cuddly kitten?"

I'm not sure what to say to that. Did she miss the man or the cat?

Gillian bursts back in. My ex has amazing timing. She does a take, but I can't read what's in her eyes.

"That was the high priestess of the Côte-Louanne coven. She's traveling here with Aurelie, the granddaughter of the woman who was high priestess when Eunice was in France. Aurelie's grandmother is too old to travel, but the coven members agreed they want to do something to see if they can help." She grabs me and engulfs me in a bosomy hug. "I'm happy for you, if something comes of this."

Gillian turns to Cassie. "She also reminded me

that before she gets here tomorrow night, we need to find out if I can make Tom shift."

She turns back to me. "Tom, do you mind? We have to know if Cassie is the only one who can control the spell. I need to try to shift you with your spell words."

I nod.

Gillian takes a deep breath, and I hold my breath, too. I'm not sure what it will mean if she can use the magic, but I'm dying to find out.

She's taking too long to say it. My hands fly up in frustration. "Well?"

She takes another deep breath and lets it out slowly. "Okay, here I go...bad Tom!"

Nothing happens. Gillian tries again, and still, nothing happens. "Oh bugger, that's not the best outcome."

I'm watching Gillian when she says it, and the worried look on her face scares me. "What's that mean?"

"I'm not sure yet. The French witches have been a tad opaque on the subject." I don't believe her. I know her well, and her expression says she knows something. She turns to Cassie and asks, "Did Eunice ever have you participate in any ritual or spell in which she passed an intimate possession of hers to you?"

"What do you mean by intimate possession?"

"Hair, skin, anything that contains living cells from her body? Or an object that you keep with you that could contain her tissue?"

"No, nothing like that. She did give me this locket, and I've worn it every day since she did," Cassie says, hooking a small golden locket out of her just-the-right-amount-of cleavage. "I guess I should probably get rid of it now. But it just has a picture of both of us inside. And I don't remember any ritual that went with it."

Gillian moves to Cassie and lifts the locket from Cassie's hand to look at it. "Could you take it off, sweetheart? I want to get a good look at what's inside."

Cassie hands it to her, and Gillian takes the locket and opens it, sliding out the portrait of Eunice on the one half and Cassie on the other. "There doesn't appear to be anything hidden under the pictures, so nothing suspicious here. I don't think the locket is anything to worry about. We'll need to figure this out later. The high priestess will want to try to determine what Eunice has done before she makes recommendations to undo it. Until then, we just sit tight."

When Cassie takes the locket back, she slips it into her pocket instead of around her neck.

*** 

High priestess Maryse—who I'd judge to be about the same age Eunice was—has an elegance which is enhanced by a soft voice and speaking only in French. I bet she was queen of the hop in her day. Aurelie, who looks to be in her mid-twenties and is built like a brick outhouse, is no slouch, either. There's something about French women. And British women. And American women. And that's why I was always in trouble when I was young.

Maybe I've grown up, because the beautiful French girl sitting on the couch across from me does nothing for me. It's not that I'm immune to her beauty, it's just that the purely sexual doesn't mean as much as it once did. I'm pretty sure the screwed up relationship I semi-agreed to with Eunice had something to do with that, whether or not I've matured.

The priestess places a few objects on a brightly colored cloth she earlier spread out on the coffee table in front of her. A stone, an arrow shaped piece of metal, some crushed herbs.

Aurelie interprets Maryse's words in her lyrical accent, "Cassie, you must sit here in front of me and place your hands on either side of the table, so..." The elder woman demonstrates by laying her own hands on the sides of the arrangement she's made. Aurelie continues to interpret as the priestess nods to Gilly. "Could you light the candles and then turn off the lights?" Gilly speaks French just fine, so the translation was meant for the rest of us.

Cassie lowers herself to the floor with her back resting on the couch between the priestess's legs.

When Gillian turns the lights off and the room is lit only by two candles, one at each end of the table, the witch places her hands on either side of Cassie's head. She speaks softly in French again. I don't know what she's saying, and Aurelie is no longer interpreting.

As she chants, Cassie begins to glow—she's enveloped by an aura that coalesces to a soft yellow which is split throughout by faint black lines, spreading like cobwebs. It's there for just an instant, then the priestess takes her hands away from Cassie's head, opens her eyes, and Aurelie tells Gillian to turn the lights back on. If Cassie could see the look on the priestess's face, I think she'd be upset.

Gillian can see the look. When she speaks, her voice broadcasts concern. "So, is there something? Is it..."

"It's no good." The priestess says through her interpreter. "She is infested with an external force that runs through all parts of her body. I believe because of the pattern I saw in her aura that it is in her blood."

Cassie gets up then. "Guys, I'm right here." She steps away and around the coffee table, to stand facing the priestess. "What's in my blood?"

The priestess nods to the younger woman, who turns to Cassie. Cassie's eyes dart from one to another as Aurelie turns the foreign words into English. "Another life essence. A piece of your grandmother. The spell responds to the living presence of the maker."

"So, freaky, right? But what does it mean?" Her eyes dart back and forth again as Aurelie interprets her question.

"It may be nothing. Was there ever a time when you and your grandmother mingled blood?"

"Actually, yeah. I was in a car accident when I was little. I needed blood, and my grandmother donated some for me."

Maryse listens quietly as Aurelie repeats what Cassie said and then replies. "That would explain it. Now, the question is—was your grandmother the kind of woman who would intentionally use a child for her own ends even if by doing so, it harmed her?"

Cassie stands there silently. I don't think she understands what the priestess is saying. But I do. I speak right up. "She would use a child, even her own grandchild, without a moment's hesitation. I don't doubt it for a minute."

The priestess looks directly into Cassie's eyes. "Then my fear is that your grandmother gave you her blood for a purpose we cannot currently guess. Witches do not donate blood. It is irresponsible. I doubt she would have done it so that she could pass her slave to you. Unless you knew about him and wanted him as yours?"

Her face flushes furiously. "No way! Sometimes I still have trouble believing any of this, and I want

Tom to be free as much as anyone."

"You must then be wary as you go through life, for the purpose of this spell has not yet shown itself. It may be that she changed her mind or that you have already fulfilled her purpose without your knowledge. Or maybe I am just a suspicious old woman. However, now that we know why you can control the shift, we can look for a pathway to undo it. In this case, I believe it fortunate you have the essence of your grandmother. It may be required to reverse or alter the spell."

Cassie nods her head and holds out her arm. "Any way I can help. Try not to bleed me dry."

Maryse smiles. "For now, I ask that you leave me with Tom," Aurelie interprets, then leaves to follow the others.

"Tom?" The priestess nods and gestures to the seat between her knees that Cassie has just vacated. "S'il vous plaît?"

***

The priestess's hands feel warm despite resting on my hair. They must be generating an unusual amount of heat. Then I feel the warmth begin to work its way through my body. I don't know if I'm generating a visible aura. I see nothing happening around me. But I feel safe, protected.

After a long period, the priestess calls to the others and she pushes at my shoulders to let me know we're done. I get up and sit across from her, but I don't rush questions at her as Aurelie comes back into the room. I get the sense she doesn't want to tell what she's learned until everyone is ready.

***

We're arranged again around the priestess in the sitting room, Cassie on the arm of my chair, Gillian in the overstuffed armchair that Cat prefers, and Aurelie next to her high priestess on the couch. She's brought her a cup of herbal tea lightened with milk. The priestess sips at it delicately before she speaks.

Aurelie interprets, "The magic which binds this man is certainly the magic of our coven's joined ones, but there are other threads contained in it— threads I do not recognize. Eunice could not have learned as much as she did within our coven. She was a novice, not the powerful witch who could have done this thing. I am not convinced that the polite young woman I knew could ever have cast this complex magic."

Gillian says, "Eunice fooled a lot of people over a long period of time. We had no idea about her until years after she'd already risen to high priestess within our coven."

I blurt out, "Yeah, yeah, yeah...Eunice was a bad person. We know that. But I need to know about me—can you undo the curse?" I immediately regret it when Maryse gives me a patient but cautioning look after Aurelie interprets my outburst to her.

"It is no curse. Instead, it is a spell to bond you with your animal brother to share his life and his experiences. The joining is a sign of respect for the beauty of the world we inhabit. In normal circumstances, you would have the power to shift yourself, and you would not need signal words. This witch corrupted the spell to give her the power but not share it with you. The only way she could have done that is to bind access to your personal power; you have no magic, yes?" I nod. She continues, "Yes, that is why you cannot shift yourself. I have no way to give you your magic back, but I believe, with Cassie's help, you can obtain the power to shift at will. I will need time to determine what must be done."

I roll that around in my head for a moment, then smile. "Better than a kick in the head, I guess." It's not like my magical powers were much to begin with. I was a poor excuse for a warlock.

Aurelie speaks now for herself. "While you were with Maryse, I explored the boundaries of this house. I had curiosity about the binding element of your spell because I am, myself, a joined one. When I leave this house, I feel a strong urge to shift. I fight off this urge, but I have access to my power, and I am strong in it. There is a very old magic that acts upon the other within and brings it to the fore. It depends on the placement of enchanted objects to draw the joined one. It is a simple thing to discover the elements of this spell and remove it. I believe this casting relies on charmed elements embedded in the walls of the house. It is a simple matter of learning where they are and then removing them."

"I could leave the house as a man?" My body tingles with adrenalin as the hope hits my bloodstream. I could go to the bar, have a beer with the boys, kick back at the beach and watch the bikini girls go by. I could go out to a movie and not have to travel there in someone's handbag.

"Man, don't tease me with this...how do we get this moving like, right now?

"Your coven's members must surround the house and perform an illumination to determine where the spelled objects are placed. When the objects are removed, you will be able to leave this house without fear of having your animal brother revealed."

"No need to wait. 'Cause I'm okay with calling all of them and waking them up right now."

She smiles a tired smile. "It is four in the morning in France. My priestess requires sleep after such a taxing day. If you could please to show us to our rooms?"

I'm souped up on adrenalin now—I could run a marathon and then turn around and run it again, but I don't have any other choice. I lead the French women up the stairs as Cassie walks Gillian to the door.

I usher Aurelie into Eunice's room where Cassie has had a new bed installed, covered now with the spare satin spread. I settle Maryse into the small but classier bedroom I've been using and which I expect she'll find more restful than the red-themed one. Cassie will be staying in the room she's had since childhood, and she says good night on the way there as we pass in the hall. She looks far away, in her own thoughts.

Downstairs again, I get comfortable on the couch under a slightly tattered quilt. Not that I sleep. How can I rest when my imprisonment may be coming to an end?

A DAY LATER, the members of the coven who know about me gather close to midnight, when the rhythms of magic fit best with the rhythms of the earth. The spell requires them to make a ring around the house. Just another tourist attraction in Giles: come see the witches in their inky robes work their spells in public!

Fortunately, what little nightlife occurs in Giles takes place on the other side of downtown. The chance of anyone walking by at this time of night is minimal. Because all the houses on the block have been converted to stores, there are few residents. Cassie and a few renters are the only ones who still live above the shops.

I turn to Cassie, "I have to go out and watch."

"Good idea. I'll go with you."

I shift as I cross the threshold while Cassie holds the front door for me to travel out into the night.

She stands by the lamp post in front, but I run a quick lap around to get an idea of what the ritual looks like. What it looks like is a B horror flick. It's not only gloomy because of the hour, but it's been cloudy all day, the wind is whipping up, and it smells like rain is on the way any minute.

The witches stand facing the house with their faces well hidden under the hoods of their robes. At first, there's light from the street lamps, but Natalie, who's at the front of the shop, raises a hand toward them and the entire string of four or five of them within lighting distance of the building wink out with a fizzling pop.

In the darkness that follows, the choir begins the chant. Quiet at first, then building. Cat's ear pick up the low hum of magic beneath their words. The witches raise their arms to each side, reaching for each other's power to share it across the space between.

A thread of gold-brown light jumps from one hand to the other, growing brighter as the chant continues. The ring entirely encloses the building now.

Maryse enters the circle and slowly walks a circuit around the house. As she passes each witch in turn, they stop chanting and slap their hands together in front. The light leaps from their fingertips to the building, settling in to illuminate small patches on the side of the house. The high priestess circles again, using a knife to pry into the wooden siding to dig out the illuminated patches that glow gold beneath. She removes a small item from each of the spots and places it into a leather pouch she wears around her neck. As she does, each patch of light fades.

After all the patches of light extinguish, the high priestess walks to Cassie and speaks in French, making a motion with her hands to her mouth, urging her with a sign to speak, then backs away from her with a gentle smile. Cassie walks over to me, where I've been sitting on the sidewalk, careful to stay out of the way. She goes down on one knee and lifts my chin so that we're looking directly into each other's eyes.

She says, "Good Tom."

And I start to shift. Outside the house, without the death of Cat to precipitate it, I shift. It's glorious. It's incredible. It's amazing.

It's a little cold.

Unfortunately, nobody thought about the problem of the lack of clothes before they decided to test the success of the casting. Natalie and some of the younger witches greet this development with whistles and catcalls. I take a bow and then strut into the house at a leisurely pace so the ladies I owe so much to can take their time admiring me. I find my robe before I run back out to the street and give that high priestess a hug she'll still be feeling on the flight back to France.

The rain, which has held off until now, begins

with a great crack of lightning, followed by the boom of thunder.

Who cares about rain? I lift my human face to it and let nature cleanse me.

While I drink my fill of raindrops, the witches break and run for the door to get out of the sudden storm. I follow them in reluctantly. Cassie is standing in the doorway, waiting.

"I didn't want to interrupt you," she says with a gigantic grin. "You were like this rain god illuminated by the lightning."

She grabs my hand and gives it a brief squeeze, then lets go and nods her head toward the door to the sitting room, where the room buzzes with the sound of excited chatter.

"Go on," I say. "I'll be there in a minute." As she heads for the hall, I turn back to the shop door, where the Egyptian cat jar perches just above on its ledge. It's easily within arm's reach for a man as tall as I am. I walk back into the rain and watch it sail through the blackness down the street. I don't see where it lands, but the sound of breaking clay is plenty satisfying.

I spend the next several minutes accepting congratulations and damp hugs from the happy band of magic-makers. I thank each of them in turn, knowing I'll be indebted to them for the rest of my life. Mere words can't thank them, but I have nothing else.

I catch sight of Gillian, standing next to Cassie,

chatting happily. She glances my way as I enter another hug, and she beams me a gorgeous smile that smoothes her skin and makes her look like the young girl I married. I'd take time to just enjoy that smile if there weren't a spider crawling up the wall behind her. Cat's becoming distracted. My eyes return to the spider's path up the wall more and more as I only half-listen to what the people around me are saying.

I see Cassie looking at me curiously as I pull my attention away from the spider and back to the conversation I've been having with a middle-aged warlock. I try to keep my eyes on him as he asks me questions about what shifting feels like, but they keep darting back to the speck still crawling up the wall. I pull back and focus on my conversation again, then the sound of a loud smack explodes through the room. Everyone turns as one.

Cassie is holding a rolled up copy of the Free Times in her hand, and there's a small black splotch where the spider used to be. She waves her hand at the group dismissively. "Carry on."

Our eyes lock, and we burst out laughing. I laugh until there are tears running from my eyes. I laugh, and I cry, like it's the first time in forty-five years.

*** 

When the partiers are gone, the French witches

have retired for the night, and Cassie is busy in the kitchen, Gillian and I start clearing up in the sitting room. When our hands brush as we both reach for the same teacup, Gillian whispers to me, "So, I'm asking again if there was a moment there between you and Cassie?"

"Maybe. I don't know. I don't know anything about emotions between normal men and women any more."

"Then Tom, you be careful. Because if you hurt that girl after everything she's done for you..."

I take her hand and look into her still beautiful and always kind eyes. "Gilly, I swear to you, I wish that I could take back everything I ever did to you and any other woman I hurt along the way. I probably deserved to be made a cat because I always acted like I was a dumb creature driven by instinct. But I learned from it. Gilly, I learned."

She studies my face. After a long moment, she replies, "Yes, I think you have."

She turns away then, scooping up a cocktail napkin from the end table before she turns back, "And Tom...I truly wish you happiness if you're able to find it. I had a wonderful life with my Martin. I can only wish the same for you."

I nod slightly. She knows I have trouble expressing sentiment, but I can see she gets that I'm grateful for her words.

KEVIN WATCHES TV, his belly spilling out of his robe, his legs open, displaying his Fruit of the Looms, his feet encased in terry-cloth house slippers. Keisha has gone home for the night. I guess he can safely be himself now.

From my perch on the window ledge, I yowl to get his attention over the drone of the TV. He looks over and jumps up, moving my direction to get a better look.

I give a heartfelt howl again, Cat's loudest, then jump off the ledge and stand in the bushes, looking up at him as he opens the window higher and peers down. I stick out my tongue and try to get Cat's face to wear a nyah-nyah-nyah look, but it's always tough to know what Cat really looks like in those situations. Cats aren't known for their range of emotions.

I turn around and shake my ass at him. We don't

want any mistakes here. He needs to know it's me. Otherwise, how will I distract him?

"For Chrissake! How did you get out of the pound?" I hear him move away from the window, cursing. I jump back to the sill, and he's running hell bent for the bedroom. He comes out fully dressed and heads for the back door. Too bad he doesn't know Cassie's hiding around the other side of the house, just waiting for me to flush him out so she can go in and find the phone he took from Cat.

Kevin comes rushing to the bushes.

From the harness hanging around my neck the words, "Good Tom," sound.

Kevin looks confused as he stands there, eyes wide, watching me change from a helpless young cat to a not-at-all helpless young man. He turns to run, but I have him in a choke-hold before he knows what's hit him.

I bend my head to his ear and talk softly. "Didn't think you'd be going up against anyone who could be a threat, now, did you? Feel more powerful with kittens or under your cloak of invisibility, do you? Too bad, because that's going to be ending very soon. Let's go into the house. That okay with you?"

Kevin nods his head. Man, I want this guy's body away from my bare skin. I drag him along in a rush. He stumbles and swears.

Cassie is on the couch with her cell phone. "That was easy to find. You should have trashed it if you didn't want me to get it back. But keeping it right on the coffee table? Seriously, were you watching the video for a sick turn-on?"

"My father will..."

"I've called your father, Kevin. He's on his way. We'll see what he'll do. Although I don't think Tom and I have much to worry about. We didn't leave the house without protection of our own. You see, Gillian's been training me."

Cassie holds a hand out toward him and rubs her thumb against her fingers. A ball of light-blue fire builds in her hand as she does. "She thinks my protection spells are every bit as good as hers now. If you want to get closer, we could test it out. I warn you, though, I put more pain into my spell than Gillian probably would have put into hers." The blue flame is suddenly shot with flares of darkness.

Kevin glares and doesn't say anything more. Right about now, I'm glad his magical abilities don't extend to laser beams shooting from his eyes.

While I hold him secure, Cassie ties Kevin's hands and feet, her flame dancing across the bonds as she does. Kevin cringes away from it.

When she's done, she says, "I was always sure that Girl Scout badge for knot-tying would come in handy one day. He's not going anywhere." With that, she gives him a solid shove in the center of the chest, and he collapses backward onto the couch.

As Cassie hands me pants and shirt to step into, she says, "And by the way, I'm pressing the send button to email the videos to a few select friends to make sure you know it can go viral fast if something happens to me or to Tom, or you just don't fulfill your side of the bargain."

"We're not making any bargains, bitch!"

When he talks to her like that, it gets my blood up, despite how calm I'd promised myself I'd stay, and I move toward him, but Cassie grabs my arm gently. "He's not worth it, remember?"

We move away for a private conversation to review one last time how we'll proceed when Robert arrives. I hear his car pull into the drive, and we glance meaningfully at each other, checking our readiness. He walks in through the unlocked back door. When he enters the living room, he takes in the situation coolly, his eyes moving from Kevin on the couch, to Cassie, and then to me.

His eyes stick on me for a long time.

"Tom. When Kevin described the man he saw on the road that night, I felt sure it had to be you. I guess I was right. However, this may not be a good time to ask how you happen to be here unchanged from the day you left."

"There are a number of changes." I reply.

We stand there a little longer, eyeing each other, then Kevin blurts out, "Jesus! Get on with it, whatever it is you're planning. I'm bored now."

Robert looks to his son, then to me again. I say, "I'll let Cassie tell you what he's been up to. Take a seat. Let's get comfortable."

Robert sits on the other end of the couch from

Kevin. I take the armchair across from him, and Cassie stands behind me, leaning on the back of the chair, close enough that I can protect her if there's a physical threat we didn't expect. And close enough that I can smell her perfume mixed with the scent of anxious sweat.

I seldom take my eyes off of Kevin as Cassie relates what we discovered and then hands the phone to Robert to view the film I'd shot. When he's done, he looks at his son with disgust.

Shaking his head, he says, "How did I raise you to be such a bastard?" He turns back to me. "What do you want me to do?"

"First, it stops. The cops didn't want anything to do with it, so you were our only choice. However he's controlling them—I think it has to do with coffee at the café spiked with one of his potions—whatever it is, that stops, too. You're mayor, so look into your police force. Second, Keisha gets a nice severance bonus and amazing references." Cassie stops and waits for an answer.

"I'll grant that," Robert says as Kevin starts to protest. "You aren't a part of these negotiations, Kevin. If you want to keep any interest in the family property, you need to keep your mouth shut."

Kevin goes silent but continues glaring at me with those psycho eyes.

"Good. Third, Kevin makes his own meals and picks up after himself from now on. He shouldn't get an opportunity to follow any more women home."

"That's a given. I'd do it without you asking for it." I'm surprised by this, but Robert seems genuine.

"Finally, Tom needs documents that say he exists and isn't in his sixties. You have access to all the forms and stamps and official documentation for the city. He needs a birth certificate that says he's Tom Sanders the Third, twenty-five years old. And we need that by the end of the week."

"I can get that. Write down the birth date you want, name of parents, and full name so that I have the details."

Cassie hands him a sheet of paper. "We're ahead of you. That should be everything you need."

"That's the last of it?"

"Yeah, that's it. Unless we find out Kevin is stalking women again. Then all bets are off."

"If he does, I'll take care of him myself. I'm surprised you don't want anything more. Eunice would have had a much longer list of demands."

Cassie's eyes flash. "I am not now, nor have I ever been, or will I ever be ANYTHING like my grandmother."

Robert just nods.

Cassie stands up. "Whatever. We're going. You can drop off the birth certificate at the shop." Man, I'm proud of her.

"You'll have it by Friday. But before you go, I need your help. Tom, could you get him out of the chair and lay him down on his stomach? Keep his arms tied, though."

"You have a reason?"

"I'm high priest. A member of my coven has abused the magic the Goddess gave him in ways that would displease her. It's my responsibility to make sure he can't do it again." Robert looks suddenly very old and very tired.

I wrangle Kevin onto the floor. He's going to have an oozy, red rug burn on his left cheek. It will be a nice complement to the now yellowing bruise below his eye.

Robert waves a hand above his head and the room is suddenly dark. He kneels with one knee on Kevin's back, holding him in place. It looks painful for both of them. He sets his right palm on his son's lower spine and closes his eyes, tilting his head upward, murmuring to the Goddess. Red magic—the color of strength and also of mercy—flows out from his hand. When the light extinguishes, he reaches a hand to me and I help him to his feet, silently.

We turn to leave, but Kevin says, "Any chance of you untying me?"

I don't even look at him. I just toss a knife from a kitchen drawer into the living room. As Robert holds the back door open for Cassie, I ask, "What did you do to him?"

"I don't know how to bind his power—that's beyond me—but he won't be able to touch anything imbued with magic without being badly burned. You have nothing to worry about from him now."

"Nuts! That's what I forgot. Hang on." I go to Kevin's room and poke around. In the top of his closet I find a paper bag that appears to be empty but has bulk and heft to it. I feel inside, and I can feel the rough fabric of a pair of coveralls. Even if he can't use magic again, which I don't fully trust, I'm not leaving it here.

When I return with the bag to the back door, Cassie and Robert are standing on the stoop, having a friendly conversation. He's her employer, after all. I'm going to have to learn to accept him.

***

"I'm so excited!" Gillian says, as she meets us at the door into the sitting room. "I could barely sit still waiting for you."

"Yeah, it's great—I get a birth certificate that matches my face instead of my age. And that bastard Kevin won't be messing with any more women without their knowledge. So, it's a good day all 'round."

"No! I mean Maryse has a way to give you the power to transform yourself. Cassie will still be able to shift you, but the magic will work as it was meant to work. You'll be able to control your own form."

I'm overcome for a moment, silent. The Cat's got my tongue, so to speak. When I recover, I can only ask, "When?"

"We're waiting for the nurse to arrive."

"Nurse?"

"It's not a ritual. You just need some of Cassie's blood. We tried to make it complicated, but in the end, it's so simple." Cassie and I follow her into the sitting room, where the French witches have turned the coffee table into an altar again. "Of course, a purification ritual beforehand is always a good idea. We are witches, after all."

Cassie teases, "Hey! I haven't agreed to this yet. Maybe I don't want to share my life essence with the guy." She pauses, making a big thing out of turning her eyes up like she's thinking. "Then again, he's the only cat I've ever had who didn't make me clean a litter box, so I suppose he deserves a reward for good behavior."

I have to admit I like it when she's sassy. Plus, she's grinning almost as broadly as I am at the news.

I'm going to be a real man again. Not a puppet for anyone. Even if Cassie went evil and tried to use the shifter magic against me, I'd be able to shift myself right back. I'd be more excited if I could separate from Cat altogether, but Aurelie already explained to me it doesn't work that way. We can't be unjoined once we've been put together. It's an even bigger commitment than marriage.

"So, does this nurse know why she's going to be moving blood from me to Tom?" Cassie asks. "Because I'd think that's kind of a strange request."

"Sweetheart, healing and witchcraft are a great mix. It's Natalie who's coming. She's retired now, but she's expert at drawing blood and giving shots. Just watch her to make sure she doesn't walk out with anything extra. I know she usually returns things later, but sometimes the kleptomania fails to amuse."

Natalie arrives, and Aurelie dims the lights. Maryse says something to her in French, and she nods. "Only Natalie, Cassie, and Tom are to stay. Gillian, you and I—would you like to go for a walk? The moon is beautiful tonight."

The high priestess completes the ritual in the candlelight. I don't understand a word she says, but I feel Cat quieting inside me as the room is cleansed of upsetting influences. It leaves such a feeling of peace, and Cassie is fully relaxed now, too. She goes from slightly pretty to stunningly beautiful in the candlelight as all the small muscles in her face relax into the calm left in the ritual's wake.

"Tom, do you know your blood type?" Natalie asks after a period of time in the calm.

"It's O positive."

"Are you absolutely sure?"

"Yes, absolutely. I donated blood several times with Gillian during the war."

"Good. And Cassie, you're the same?"

"Yes. And that's a definite, too."

"Good, that means there's little risk of danger from the transfusion. However, I want someone to keep an eye on you for twenty-four hours afterward—no running out to the bars, understand? I'm only moving a few drops of blood over, but I need to know if anything unusual happens over the next day."

I nod obediently. This is a side of Natalie I haven't seen before. She's surprisingly competent. "Absolutely. No running to the bars. I'll just get falling-down drunk right here."

Cassie rolls her eyes as Natalie swabs the skin on her inner elbow with alcohol.

"Ready?" Natalie asks as she positions Cassie's arm. Cassie nods and turns her head away, then Natalie eases the needle in. She must have done a good job. Or maybe Cassie is braver than I am about needles. She doesn't react at all. Her bright-red blood flows up into the syringe and Natalie removes it, pressing a cotton ball against the bead of blood that tries to flow away.

Then, it's my turn. Natalie slides the needle into my arm after preparing it with alcohol. I wince when cooling blood mixes with my own. Not a comfortable sensation.

When it's done, Natalie cleans up and packs up. It feels ordinary. Not what I expected at all.

"Well, dumbass, are you going to say it?" Cassie blurts out.

"Don't say the words. Think them only. The signal words must be held secret. None of you must speak of this. The magic of my coven must be protected so that it is never corrupted again," the high priestess says in slow, careful English that none of us knew she understood until that minute. That's a surprise. Who knows what all that interpreting was about. Sheesh. Witches.

We murmur agreement.

"Then use your inner voice, Tom Sanders, brother of my coven."

I take a moment to mentally prepare myself for the pain, and then I think the words. Cat pushes his way out of me as I draw into him. Somehow, the pain is barely there. Maybe because, for the first time, no part of me is fighting the change. I allow myself and Cat to truly be one. I crawl out from under my shirt, and I'm happy to be walking lightly across the floor on his tiny, padded feet.

Cat finds his way to Cassie's legs and winds his way around them, purring and rubbing his head against her in thanks. He's expressing the thing I don't know how to say—my gratitude for the gift she gave me.

She reaches down and scratches behind my ears briefly. I have a feeling if she knew how that feels for me, she'd be embarrassed she did it in public.

Gillian and Aurelie come in the back door, and Maryse calls to them to join us. Cassie sits in the big armchair. I jump into her lap and think good Tom.

I grab a pillow to preserve what's left of my modesty, but everyone's laughing so hard I don't think Cassie minds having a lapful of naked me.

CAT SHIFTS TO TOM, and I've got a lap full of undiluted man. My brain can't decide if it's thrilled or mortified, but my body is voting for thrilled. Gillian and Aurelie have just come in, so everybody gets to witness his little joke. I laugh with them, though. With everything I've learned since Granny died, I can't get uptight about unimportant things any more. Plus, I do have a lapful of naked Tom, so everyone has to be thinking, 'Wow! Lucky Cassie.'"

Omigod! Tom has control over his shifting, and he can leave the house! I want to kiss him with joy for what's happened, but there are way too many people hanging around. You should never kiss a naked man in front of his ex-wife and a roomful of elderly ladies.

Gillian stops laughing first and gets Tom's robe. She tosses it to him, and everyone except Natalie politely looks away as he drops his privacy pillow and leverages himself off the arm of the chair to get decent. Once he's in his robe, he excuses himself to grab his heap of clothes and get dressed again in the bathroom.

The atmosphere careens from ritual to party, but with half the guests being over sixty, it quiets down pretty fast. Gillian and Natalie take their leave after Maryse heads up the stairs on Aurelie's steadying arm. Tom and I are alone.

Tom goes to the kitchen and starts rattling around. As I pack up the candles and candlesticks from the cleansing ritual, Tom flips the light switch off with his elbow on the way into the room, He has a glass of wine in each hand. I retrieve a candle I've just put away and light it again.

He hands me a glass, and I sit back in the big overstuffed chair, looking at him over the candle flame as he sips at his wine.

"Hard to believe that wine comes in a box these days. What will they think of next?"

I shrug. When did wine not come in a box?

"You know, I can get my own place as soon as Robert gets me that birth certificate if you want me to. From there, I can get a social security number, and even a passport." He keeps his eyes on my face the whole time. He says it, but he doesn't seem eager to move out.

"Yeah, I know you can." The thought of him not being here makes me sad. Then again, I'm not sure if it's because I'll miss Cat snuggling up next to me or laughing and teasing with Tom over breakfast. The living situation has been pretty weird.

"Do you want me to go?"

"No."

"Do you want me to stay?"

"I don't know. The idea of you and Cat not being here..." I try not to give too much away, but I think I'm probably blushing. The tips of my ears are hot.

"I might try to downplay the whole Cat part of my future relationships. It's not exactly a trump card for most people."

Then I get this hope that he's hinting toward the thing that's making me blush and ask, "So, do you mean like male/female stuff, like you and me, because..."

Tom looks tired all of a sudden. I'd forgotten that despite his jokes and bravado, he was basically my evil grandmother's sex toy for half a century. I can't keep wallowing in my own hurt over Dan and thinking sexy Tom could be a convenient painkiller. Despite the lusty stuff, I think I really care about him. We've been through a lot together. "Whatever happens, Tom, there's enough room for the three of us here, I think, as long as Cat doesn't insist on bringing his girlfriends around."

We sit there, quietly sipping our wine until Tom stands up, walks over to me, and kisses me on the top of the head. Like I'm his daughter or something.

With that fatherly kiss, I suddenly feel like I've been completely on the wrong page about what I thought might be going on between us: have I been reading the signs through wishful-thinking-colored glasses? What was he doing naked in my lap, then?

But he doesn't move away, just leaves his hands there on my shoulders, his mouth still touching my hair. I tip my head back to look at him. Our eyes meet, and our lips meet, and my heart lurches wildly inside my chest. Tom's hands move to my hair, stroking it softly as our mouths slide tentatively together, mine opening against his gently probing tongue, until he finally pulls away, leaving me breathless.

He steps back and announces, "Thank you. Thank you for teaching me how not to be alone...I'm...I'm going out to hunt." And just like that, he's a cat, and I'm watching his furry little butt disappear through the open window.

I go to bed as soon as Tom leaves because the wine and the activity of the day and the confusion left by that kiss have worn me out. I wake to the sound of purring an hour or two later. Cat is sitting in the velvet bedside chair, preening himself with his claws outspread, his pink tongue making a rhythmic, orderly circuit of each of his toes in turn.

I reach out my hand and Cat's head rubs against it, putting an end to his grooming session. He jumps down from the chair, and disappears through the doorway. It seems Tom just stopped in to let me know that everything is okay.

Maybe we'll talk about that kiss tomorrow.

IT'S SO AWKWARD at breakfast. I can't believe how the easy relationship we'd begun to develop changed so much over one little kiss. Tom is quiet and thoughtful. He keeps looking at me strangely. I don't know what he's thinking, and finally I just have to blurt it out as he slips a perfectly cooked piece of French Toast onto my plate.

"Tom, talk to me. Why did you leave last night? There wasn't anything wrong with what we did."

"No, Cass. We didn't do anything wrong. But I shouldn't have kissed you. I've tried to be honest with you, but it's been so long since I was human, I don't always remember how."

I smile at him then. "I think you're doing a good job. Better than a lot of guys I've known."

"I'm not going for just 'better than a lot of guys'. I owe so much to you and to Gillian, and to all the witches who helped me out with no questions asked. For all of you, I need to be the best man that I can. And that means coming clean about something that affects you."

"Is it about Granny? Because unless I'm actively in danger, that can wait. I've got more than enough surprises about her to sort through right now. Feel free to hold off on any more for a while."

"No, you'll want to know this. It's about Dan as much as it's about Eunice. That night—the night you found Dan with that other woman…"

"Yeah, my supposed best friend."

"It was a big surprise, right?"

"Duh."

"Did you feed Dan and this girl anything Eunice made you?"

"Just those refrigerator pickles Dan liked. I could never stand them. But both of those guys ate tons of them at dinner."

"Right," he says, "And then those two people ended up in bed together just before your wedding. A wedding your grandmother wanted to make sure never took place."

"What do you mean? Gran liked Dan."

"No, she didn't," he insists. "And she didn't want you to marry him or anyone. You know she wanted you to move to Giles and help her in the shop."

"Yeah, but…"

"And where are you now?"

I think about what he's saying. If he's right, I

blamed two of the people I love the most in the world for something they had no control over. "Tom, omigod, if that's true..."

"You need to talk to Dan." I see fear in his eyes as he says it. At first, I'm not sure what that means, then I realize he's got to be afraid I won't want him hanging around if I have a man in my life. He's afraid he'll be alone again.

"Tom...no matter what happens, you're staying here, right? I wouldn't throw you out."

His stiff shoulders relax. "Thank you, but even if I couldn't stay, I'd still tell you. It's the right thing to do. I'd seen Eunice throw a monkey wrench between people before. She was good at it."

"Wow! She used me to deliver the spell. She knew I was making dinner for both of them as soon as I got back home. How is it even possible that I just kept falling into her traps for all those years? Was anything she ever said to me genuine?"

I feel myself getting angry, really angry at Granny Eunice for the first time since she died. I may have a lot of stuff still left to deal with now that most of the weirdness is over.

Tom doesn't answer. What could he say? He gives me a sad smile. Then he goes back to dusting the shelves.

I'm immersed in my own thoughts when Robert walks in, an envelope in his hand. He comes toward me, and Tom is instantly at my side. To say his movements were cat-like would be an understatement. He practically teleported there from across the shop.

"Tom," says Robert, "I have something for you."

I take out my phone and incline my head toward the hall, "Okay if I duck out to make a call?"

Tom nods.

When I return to the shop, Robert's gone, Tom's staring at the new birth certificate he holds in his hands, and I'm feeling kind of buoyant.

Dan's coming. He's on his way right now.

*** 

Gillian bustles into the shop just as I'm flipping the sign to closed for lunch hour. She air kisses Tom on her way in and then hands me a nicely wrapped package. In her other hand, she carries a bag from the café.

"Housewarming gift for you two. Come on, let's have some lunch, and you can open your surprise."

I set out plates and Gillian pulls out three roast beef sandwiches on thick slices of crusty bread, but who can think of eating when there's an unopened present in the room?

"Now, before you open your gift, just let me say that I went to absolutely no expense or bother. It's something that I've had around the house that I think more appropriately belongs in yours now. Tom, I thought about returning Polly to you, but I don't think she'd adapt very well at her age to a new home even if you are her old master. And with Martin gone, I appreciate the company, even if the conversation is severely limited. But you will recognize the gift, so go ahead."

I look at Tom to see if it's okay to start tearing into the wrapping and he nods. I rip away and then lift off the lid of the box. Inside is an antique quilt. I look at Tom, waiting for a cue. I'm not sure what to say, but Tom steps in quick enough.

"My mother's quilt. It's as beautiful as I remember. Thank you for keeping it all these years. I'll insist that Cassie use it on her bed in thanks for everything she's done for me."

Gillian looks confused. "Oh? Did I get things wrong? I thought when you said you'd be living here together..."

We both shake our heads. Tom explains. "No. We're not together that way. And you may be seeing Cassie's Dan around, if things turn out the way we expect. He's coming for lunch in a few minutes and Cassie was going to go out, but maybe you and I could go instead and leave them these sandwiches and a nice warm quilt just in case they need one? I've got a paycheck. I can afford to buy a lady a lunch."

Gillian looks surprised but recovers. "All right, Tom. I'll take you up on that. Who am I to stand in the way of young love?"

I feel kind of giddy, thinking that maybe it really could be young love again, after all. I guess I'm okay with Tom brushing off my awkward crush, although I'm still wondering what that kiss was all about. He and Gillian head out the back, but in a moment, he returns and ushers Dan into the kitchen. "Look who I found on my way out." And then he's gone.

Dan and I stand there at loose ends, just sort of looking at each other after saying hi. Then we both say, "I missed you."

We sit across the table from each other and talk for the first time since the day I walked in on him and Charlie together.

I STILL LAUGH SO EASILY with Gilly. What could I have been thinking when I first wandered off for some slap and tickle with Eunice and ended up losing my freedom in the end? Just talking about old times brings them back, and I still see the girl in her, the spark of youth.

I reach across the table at the café and take her hand. I smile at her, that smile she always said she couldn't resist. Cassie says that being back with Dan won't change things, but I know it will. I'll be deserted, and I'm desperate to avoid feeling so alone again. Gillian pulls her hand gently away. "Don't be ridiculous, Tom. I'm old enough to be your grandmother now. Just stop."

"Can't we hold hands and act stupid like we used to for old times sake?"

"You know we can't. I was foolish enough to marry a stunted boy-man once, but my youthful days of stupidity are well out of my system. Everything's different now. Everything. What do you think the other people in this restaurant see when you smile at me that way? You'll put them off their lunch."

"But you still love me. I know you do. I feel it when you look at me."

"I love the memory, Tom. That's all. Once you get to a certain age, those memories are friendly ghosts. But you don't necessarily want to live with ghosts."

"But I'm not a ghost. I'm a man." I give her my most charming grin again. "Or a cat. Or both. But I'm not a ghost."

She stands up and shakes her head. "I'm sorry, Tom. I really am. I know you're lonely. I'd hoped that you and Cassie would find each other—I was so sure you had, based on the looks you two pass back and forth. I don't understand why you'd push her back to a man who treats her as badly as Eunice did. I'll never understand you, Tom." She puts money on the table for her uneaten lunch and then walks out.

I follow her out to the street, baffled. "What do you mean, a man who treats her like Eunice did? Eunice did something to him to make him cheat on her. I know she did. I watched her send the pickles home with Cassie."

She turns and looks at me. "What? Refrigerator pickles? Tom, sometimes a pickle is just a pickle.

Dan has never treated her with respect. The last time they were here, I caught him giving his cell number to one of the waitresses in the café while Cassie was helping out Eunice in the shop. I was going to tell her, but then they broke up and I didn't have to."

Wish I'd known that this morning. See what happens when you don't get out much? "Oh man, Gilly, I screwed up. And I thought I was doing the right thing!" I turn and make a beeline for the shop.

How could I be so stupid?

\*\*\*

I blast through the back door and hustle into the kitchenette, but there's no one there. The quilt's gone, too. Damn it all! I'm too late. Anything I say now is only going to hurt her.

I sneak quietly up the stairs, hoping I don't barge in on a private moment. Her bedroom door is open. I move in silence, the way Cat's taught me, and peek around the doorframe. There's no one there.

"Tom?" Cassie says, coming out of the bathroom behind me. "Why are you sneaking around up here? Did you and Gilly have a fight?"

I turn. Why do I feel like I've been caught playing hooky? "No…I…she…where's Dan?"

"Dan's an ass! He started right in with 'sell up and come back to Boston, baby. Think of the cool car you could buy me with that extra cash.' Not a word of acknowledgement about how he hurt me. And then he gets a call, and Charlie's face comes up on his phone, and he's all like, 'I have to get this'. Suddenly I knew the pickles had nothing to do with it." She walks past me and sits heavily on the edge of the bed, turning to the side to face me. "I was such a jerk. I didn't want to see what was right in front of my eyes all that time."

"I'm sorry."

"No, it's good," she says. "I'm glad it happened. I doubted myself for leaving him before, but now I know it was the smart thing to do. It's about time for me to start seeing things clearly." She smiles and pats the bed. "I also think it's time we talk about that kiss, don't you?"

I sit next to her, not sure what to expect. I was never much of one for talking about feelings, and the only other time I've felt stirrings like I feel for Cassie was with Gillian. It would be difficult to forget how well that turned out. I sit primly, waiting for her to talk.

She reaches for both of my hands where they lay folded in my lap and turns them over, smoothing my palms with her thumbs. Shyly, under her breath, she says, "I didn't mean we'd actually talk, Tom."

Oh.

She leans in to me, her mouth tantalizing close to mine and whispers, "But we should probably take it slow."

So we do. We share a long, slow kiss. A kiss that

takes all day and most of the night. We memorize each other's bodies with our hands and our mouths, mentally recording the sounds of each other's joy for the moments when we'll have to be away from each other, already knowing it will be a long time before we let that happen.

Cassie gets dressed in the morning for a few minutes to write a sign that says, "Closed for Renovations" and stick it in the front window of the shop. It isn't a lie. We're tearing down faulty foundations and building a home for each other with loving whispers and hope.

# Epilogue

I HAVE TO HUNT eventually. I can't go much longer without giving Cat some freedom. Cassie understands, and we both agree that we should open up the shop in the morning and get used to other people again. It's been three days now.

I slip back in an hour later. Cassie isn't in bed where I left her. I wander through the house looking for her. Not downstairs. Not upstairs. I call out, hearing the frantic tone in my own voice. Where is she? I worry every day that we haven't seen the last of Kevin.

Then, I hear her a faint scuffling sound from above. The attic? What would she be doing in the attic at this hour of the night?

I climb the narrow stairs that feel much less claustrophobic when Cat is prowling for mice. In the dim, dusty space, Cassie's going through a box of Eunice's junk with her earbuds firmly shoved into her ears. I relax.

"Hey," I yell, getting her attention. She plucks the music out of her ears and looks at me expectantly. "You're decluttering in the middle of the night?" I ask, from where I stand on the top stair.

"I don't know, I woke up, and I had a lot of energy for some reason..." She smiles and shrugs her shoulders. She can get this way after we make love—bright and full of get-up-and-go. She looks radiant, innocent, and yet so sexy in her plain, cotton nightie. "It's time I get rid of the rest of Granny's stuff. I can face it now. I've got you, and I've got Gillian, and I'm so much stronger than I ever knew. Anyway, some of this stuff is really cool. I think Eunice stored her own mother's things up here. I found this beautiful old brooch just thrown into the bottom of a box."

She raises the brooch and opens the pin on the back to put it on her nightgown, but I call out, "Cass! We need to know if there's anything dangerous up here before you go putting on brooches. Any of this junk could be spelled, and we wouldn't be able to tell. We need to get Gillian or Natalie up here to check it out."

"You know what? You're right." She puts the brooch down on top of a box, then something else catches her eye. She reaches out for it.

"Oh wow, this is interesting..."

I step up onto the landing to get a better look, stooping under the low ceiling. She's holding a clay box with what must once have been bright paint decorating it. I recognize the symbols. They're Egyptian: life, death, reincarnation. Something Eunice must have collected because of her Egypt obsession, like the canopic jars and archeology magazines. Cassie reads the symbols aloud in English. How could she know the words? A feeling of dread takes hold of me. I yell and bolt toward her to smack it out of her hand, but it's too late.

Blue-gray smoke bursts from the vessel and engulfs her, then enters her body through her mouth and nose. Her posture changes. She turns to me, stiffly, with that Daughters of the American Revolution formality.

Cassie's playful look has been replaced by one that I know too well. It's cruel and controlling. It's Eunice. I back away instinctively.

"Hello Tom," she says. "Have you been making time with my granddaughter? Have you been bad, Tom?"

The cat appears as the man shrinks away.

# ABOUT THE AUTHOR

Jill Nojack is a writer, musician and artist. The Bad Toms Series is her second published series.. The Familiar was selected for publication by readers through the Kindle Scout program. The digital version of this book is traditionally published on the Kindle Press imprint.

When she isn't exploring her creative side, Jill enjoys laughing too loud and long in public, long bike rides, and talking about herself in third person. She resides in the great American Midwest with a long-suffering cat and makes her living as a computer tech, because, if you're lucky, that's what you do with degrees in English and Sociology.

You can visit www.jillnojack.com for more information about the series along with Jill's other books. You can also sign up for the email newsletter if you would like to be notified when new books in this and her other series are released.